Where the Mountain Meets the Sky

By Travis Heady

May God lead you on your own journey. I hope this book is an encouragement along the way.

Travis Heady

Thanks and Acknowledgements

First of all, I want to thank my daughter Bethany. She was the first to encourage me to write this book, and was my biggest champion all along the way. I also want to thank my wife Heather and my other daughters Megan and Sierra for all of their encouragement, feedback, and support all along the way. Furthermore, I want to thank Canyon Ridge Baptist Church, where this story was originally born as a series of dramatic sermons, and home to many wonderful people who cheered for me through this process. Thanks to my Dad, Michael Heady, for his editing and critique. And finally, thanks to Jesus, about whom I intend for this book to really be about. My prayer is that you will experience your own relationship with him grow through the reading of Where the Mountain Meets the Sky.

Of course, neither the ideas in the book nor my growing understanding of God were birthed in a vacuum. Among others, I wish to acknowledge two works that had a profound effect on my me, without which this book would never have come to be: He Loves Me! Learning to Live in the Father's Affection, by Wayne Jacobsen (Windblown Media) and The Cure: What If God Isn't Who You Think He Is And Neither Are You by John Lynch, Bruce McNicol and Bill Thrall (Cross Section Ventures, Inc). Not only do I recommend these two books to my own readers, but I want to give credit where credit it due.

Chapter 1 – The Maze

Life is a journey. It sounds cliché, I know, but it is the best way to describe this life as I have experienced it. Looking back, I can see that every choice I made was like a path, chosen from a multitude of paths, with no clear view of where it would lead me and no way of going back. It sounds like a precarious way to live, I know. For a long time, what I wanted most was a map that would show me the way. Now I believe there is no map. Instead, what I have found is a guide. This guide is not content for me to tell him where I wish to go and he takes me there, though. Instead, he leads me where he wants me to go. It certainly takes some getting used to, and even now it can be quite unnerving sometimes, but it is also the most freeing, joyful experience I could ever imagine. The key is that I learned to live out of the truth that my guide loves me. It's amazing how much of my life I spent never feeling as though I was loved by another person, even when I was blazing good trails.

It was a long road that I took before I met my guide though, and another long road before I realized that I actually could trust him and his paths. I certainly would not presume to tell you that I trust him perfectly now, but I recognize that my lack of trust is usually what leads me into trouble.

I think that I am already beginning to ramble a little bit, and so it would probably be best if I just tell you my story, the story of my journey.

I will start with the point in my life that I really set out on my own path. Of course, growing up, I had already had many adventures and experiences that helped to make me the young man that I was. But through those years, I was still on the paths that my parents chose, only taking little side trails along the way.

When it was finally time to head out on my own, I packed up my backpack full of all the things that seemed to define me. I went carefully through each of them as I put them into the large backpack, and I was surprised to see how quickly it filled up. There didn't seem to be much room for new experiences, but I guess our backpacks grow and change over time to accommodate for it.

Some of the things in my backpack during those early days were great things to have with me, like the good values my parents had taught me and the education I had received. But some of the things I wished I could forget about and just throw away, because they were bad experiences of pain or doubt that came when others abused me or I had made a poor choice.

Many of the things in my pack did not fall clearly into either category though. They contained elements of both. For example, there was an experience I had in school that stayed with me for a long time. It came out of the excitement and wonder that I had as a kid – I knew from a young age that I wanted to be an adventurer and explorer when I grew up. One of my teachers would always give us these creative writing journal assignments, which I usually hated because I would rather be outside, exploring or playing some game with my friends. But one day the topic she gave was, "A faraway place that I hope someday to visit…"

My imagination took off, and I began to write feverishly in my journal. I didn't settle for some silly, local place like the ocean or polar ice cap. Instead, I chose Alpha Centauri, the closest star system to our sun. I know – "Nerd Alert!" But it is only 4.3 light-years away, and I thought of how exciting it would be to travel through space and explore new planets and stars that literally no one had ever been to before. It was a good memory, until it was tainted a few weeks later when a boy in the class stole my journal, found that entry, and read it aloud to the class while laughing at my foolishness. The teacher did nothing to stop him, and I learned not to let my dreams get so big, or at least not to let others know what they were.

By the time I had my backpack filled and heaved it over my shoulders, I was shocked at how heavy it was. Some of the things in there just really weighed me down. But what could I do about it? "It is what it is," I reasoned, so I would just have to get stronger and learn to live with it.

And off I went, with a pocket full of dreams, as the saying goes. Like I said, I wanted to be an explorer, so I had been listening intently to people my whole life when they talked about exotic and exciting places that they had visited. Oceans and beaches, forests and rivers, and even jungles were all just waiting for me. All I had to do was find the right trails and I was there! But the place I wanted to visit most was the mountains. I had seen pictures that others had taken and I could hardly wait to see them firsthand, rising up before me. Someone I had overheard talking with my parents had even said that the mountains were where you could find God, and that sounded like an amazing adventure to me! I didn't know if they meant it literally, or if it was one those metaphors adults sometimes use to describe something remarkable, but either way I figured I wanted to experience it for myself.

But of course, I didn't know the way. I didn't have a map. So I just figured I would have to wing it, and see where the trails took me.

I had only been travelling for a short while when I came to my first major obstacle. I hadn't even come to any forks in the trail when I suddenly had to stop because the path just ended. There was a vast canyon in front of me where the trail should have been. I could see the trail pick up again on the other side, and I thought I might actually have been able to see the mountains rising up in the distance! I had no idea they would be so close. But first I had to deal with this canyon. I examined it carefully, looking first for a bridge and then for a trail leading down, but there was nothing to be found. Instead, about six feet below the rim of the canyon, a mist covered everything below as far as I could see. There was also a stench rising up out of the depths. It reminded me of the smell of a bloated dead animal I had once found as a child.

As I stared across the dark expanse, I decided to name this place, "The Abyss." It was much more daunting than a simple canyon. And there was no way I could traverse this Abyss. After several minutes of fruitless searching, I was starting to despair. But I refused to give up so easily, and told myself not to give up. There was no going back, after all. So instead I started to explore the edges on either side of me. And that's when I saw a crude, hand-painted sign with an arrow on it nailed to a tree. The sign said, "Find your own way," and the arrow pointed off to one side along the edge of the Abyss. I made my way through the trees about a dozen yards, and sure enough, there was a trailhead there, with a clearly marked and even paved trail leading off into the trees. It made a sharp bend about one hundred yards up, so I couldn't see where it was going. It sure seemed like the best option though, so I took it.

Off I went, but as soon as I made the bend I discovered that things were not as clearly marked as I had hoped. The trail quickly had a fork in it, and another, and another, choices going in all directions. And the trees started to crowd closer and closer to the trail. I chose one path, then another. I tried to remember where I'd come. Right, left, left, right, straight where there was a "T", and so on. But it quickly got confusing and I gave up.

After walking for half an hour or so, I realized that at some point the trees had been replaced by concrete walls, rising up twenty and even thirty feet on both sides. The concrete walls had trees painted on them. That must be why I didn't notice the change at first. The light was dreary and dark. When I peered upwards, over the walls, everything looked cloudy and dark. Walls and various paths were everywhere, going in all directions –suddenly the realization hit me like a punch in the stomach - I was in a maze! I had unwittingly entered a vast labyrinth and I had no idea where I had come from or where I was going. "Finding my Own Way" was going to be harder than I thought. And already my heavy pack was really weighing me down.

I came across some other people for the first time since I had entered the maze. It was two women who had built a make-shift canopy out of what looked like an assortment of old clothes and linens in a corner where two walls met. The two women looked impoverished, and sat motionless under their canopy with their eyes down. I wondered why they had stopped instead of continuing to look for a way through the maze, but I didn't say anything. Neither did they, and I passed by them without incident.

As I walked on and on and on, I began to notice some very strange things about the maze. The path looked smooth and flat, but it always felt like I was walking uphill! At first I thought it must be my imagination, but I couldn't shake the feeling. Even if I turned around to go back the way I had come, it felt like I was going up a steep incline. I always thought my grandfather was joking about going uphill both ways! Then I came to a straight stretch that felt like I was climbing hundreds and hundreds of steps, even though the path looked level and smooth. It was very strange.

I began to pass more and more people the farther I went into the maze. Some looked like they knew exactly where they were going, striding purposefully forward with their eyes locked straight ahead. Some looked as lost as I was beginning to feel, aimlessly wandering first in one direction and then another. Others, like the two women, had stopped and made a camp in a corner of the walls here and there. Nobody seemed to be talking with anyone else, and nobody would make eye contact with me. I actually tried to stop a few people who looked confident in what they were doing, but they ignored me went on their way.

So I kept walking. What else was I supposed to do? Left, left, right, straight, then left again. I had been walking for hours now, and my pack was really heavy. It was all I could think about, not knowing if I would ever find any direction in this labyrinth. Then, I came around a bend to see a wider courtyard in front of me. In the middle of it was a booth, with a sign over it that read, "Information". "Finally… some answers," I thought. There was a long line, so I jumped into it immediately.

After a few minutes, I decided to try to talk to the person standing in front of me in line. It was a young woman wearing khaki shorts and a T-Shirt with her brown hair pulled up in a tight ponytail. She was staring down at a small notebook full of scribbles and hand-drawn diagrams. "Hi," I say. "How's it going?"

"Oh, fine. I'm fine," the young woman replied, looking up. I got the distinct impression that she had not even realized I was there until I said something.

"Good. So, what is this place?" I asked. "I've only been here a little while."

"Well, "she said, closing her notebook. "It's like this. There are lots of different paths you can go, depending on what you want to do in your life. I don't think it really matters as long as you find a path that you like."

"Oh," I answered, not sure if I really understood any better than I had before. "And how do I know if I will like a path or not? How will I know where it will take me?"

"Oh, I think they all end up at the same place," she stated matter-of-factly. "It's more about enjoying the journey than worrying about the destination. I hear there is a beautiful valley where we can all have whatever makes us happy, all day long, forever, and that's where the paths end up. But I haven't found anybody that's ever actually been there. As for choosing a path, just try one for awhile, and if you don't like it you can always switch. Just try to stay away from the eastern part of the maze."

"Why? What's over there?" I asked.

"That's where the edge of the dark chasm is. You know what that chasm is, don't you?"

I shook my head.

"It's death! The end. No more paths. No more Beautiful Valley. You don't want to go there."

I agreed wholeheartedly. I had no intention of going anywhere near that Abyss if I could help it. Then the girl was up to the information booth, and I realized I hadn't even asked her what her name was. I could hear her asking about the "Path to Spiritual Awakening" and saw the guide pointing towards the left, and with that she was gone.

I stepped up to the booth. "May I help you?" the guide asked without looking up at me. She was a short, middle-aged woman with glasses and an untidy mop of light brown hair. Her attention was focused almost entirely on the puzzle book laid open in front of her.

"Um...I don't know which path to take," I mumbled.

She glanced up at me with an extremely irritated expression on her face. "Well, it depends on where you want to go."

"I guess I don't know where I want to go," I admitted.

"Then I guess it doesn't matter which path you take, does it? Next!"

"Wait!" I interjected quickly. "Do you have a map or something?"

"No maps," she stated, looking back down at her book. "Next!"

"Which way is east?" I asked hurriedly. She pointed towards the left and my turn was over.

Back on my own, I decided to go west, away from the Abyss. I tried to keep up with which way east was and kept it behind me, but it was hard with all the twists and turns of the maze. If I didn't know better, I would have thought all of the paths were turning me east, but that couldn't possibly be true.

It seemed like I walked for days and days. "Maybe years, who knows?" I thought to myself. My backpack was unbelievably heavy, and the dreariness of the maze was starting to make be depressed. The air was hot and stuffy. The perpetually cloudy sky made everything look dim and lifeless. Where were the beaches? Where were the jungles? Everything was the same, no matter which way I went. I was getting very discouraged. Why couldn't I find a good path to follow? Why couldn't I find this Beautiful Valley that the girl had told me about? Why couldn't I find something to give me direction? This was not at all what I had in mind when I dreamed of being an explorer.

I walked over to a wall and sunk down against it. Now I understood why some people had stopped and made camp where they had. How long had they been in the maze? I certainly wasn't ready to give up, but I desperately wanted something to give me direction, to give me hope.

"Been walking long?" I heard a voice to my left say, and I realized with a start that I was not alone. Squatted down on a thread worn blanket was an old man. His cowboy boots looked like they had seen more miles than I had walked in my entire life, and his stained blue jeans were full of holes. His heavy brown jacket and flannel shirt looked warm, if just as old as the rest of his outfit, but I couldn't help but wonder why he was wearing them in the stifling heat of the maze. What really drew my attention, besides his scraggly white beard, was the large straw cowboy hat he wore low over his eyes.

"Hello," I managed to say, still feeling awkward at this impromptu meeting. "I didn't see you there. Sorry."

"Nothing to be sorry for. Most folks just mosey right on by without noticing me."

"Yeah," I grinned slightly. "I've noticed that about 'most folks' too."

The old man scooted himself over next to me without getting up. "But you didn't answer my question. How long have you been here?"

"I'm not entirely sure," I admitted. "It's hard to tell how much time has gone by in here. I think it must have been several days."

"Oh, well, you're just a pup then," the man chuckled. "Tell me how tired you are when it's been several years, or even decades."

"Is that how long you've been in here?" I asked, dismayed. "Can't you find a way out?"

"Nope. To be honest with you, I gave up on that years ago. I don't think there is a way out."

His words felt like iron weights falling onto my shoulders. No way out? How could that be? This couldn't be all that life had to offer! It just couldn't.

He could tell what affect his words had on me, and the old man grinned. I could see a large gap where his front teeth should have been. "It's not that bad, Son, really. I reckon there are some good things in the maze, too."

"Like what?" I asked. "I haven't seen anything but walls and more walls."

"Oh, well, I guess I thought maybe you hadn't seen them yet," he said flatly, and then started to laugh loudly at his own joke. I couldn't help but join him. It was the first light-hearted moment of pure enjoyment I had experienced in a very long time.

Finally, when he had calmed down, he leaned forward and said, "C'mon, I want to show you something." With that he slowly stood up, moved back over to his blanket, and heaved his own backpack over his shoulders. It was just as threadbare as the rest of him, and I noticed that he had a limp when he walked.

We moved slowly around a few bends in the maze and came to a dark path with caution tape stretched across the entrance. The old man smiled conspiratorially at me, again showing the gap in his teeth, and then gradually bent himself low enough to slip under the tape. I followed him, curious as to what the mysterious path would lead.

It wasn't long until I realized why the caution tape had been put up. Something had happened here, long ago by the looks of it, to damage the path. There were cracks in the path, and chunks of concrete fallen from the walls littered the ground. The old man carefully navigated the way, avoiding loose debris and fallen obstacles.

"I used to come down here all the time," he confided, "when I was younger and had more of a git-ee-up in my step."

It was obvious that the old man knew the path well, moving instinctively to one side where a pit had formed on the other and squeezing through rocks that I had thought closed off when I first saw them.

We came around another bend and there was a huge pile of broken concrete blocking the path forward.

"This is as far as I can come, anymore," he said sadly. "A few years ago, I took a nasty fall from up there and wrenched my knee. Now I can't climb like I used to. But what I want you to see it up there." He pointed up towards the top of the pile, probably fifteen feet above us. "You go on now, and get yourself up there so you can see better."

I hesitated for a moment, not wanting to leave the old man and not sure how safe the climb was. But soon curiosity got the better of me, and I began to climb. It was not an easy climb, especially with my heavy backpack pulling me back, but after a few minutes I had reached the highest point that I could climb to. Above me, rocks and gravel had completely blocked the trail. I looked back down at the old man expectantly.

"OK, now move over to your right," he called up. Once I had done so, he said, "Now lean down and look between that large rock on your left and the one below it."

I bent down and peered through the dark gap between the two rocks. Only it wasn't dark! When I had lined my head up with the gap just right, I could see a space on the other side of the debris. There, about thirty yards away, was a space where the wall had crumbled, and a gap appeared between the remains of the wall and the clouds overhead. In other words, there was a square of bright, blue sky and sunshine shining in! It was the most beautiful thing I had seen since entering the maze.

"Wow," I muttered, and just stared longingly at the blue sky for the longest time.

"It's really something, isn't it?" the old man called up from down below. "I wish I could still climb up there to see it."

Finally, I scrambled back down to where he waited for me. "Thank you," I said, breathless. "What do you think is out there?"

"Well, now, that's the question, isn't it? There's not really a good way to get over there. No way out, but it sure is pretty to see. In fact, I like to think of it as a little gift from God to help me keep going. Or I did, until I couldn't get up there to see it anymore."

"What do you know of God? I asked, curious.

"Never met him. But I like to think he's out there somewhere, watching over us and helping out where he can. Who knows, maybe we'll find him if we ever find our way out of this stinking maze!"

We walked back out of the restricted area in silence. When we came back to where I had first met the old man, he turned to me and said, "Well, I reckon this is goodbye. There's nothing for me around these parts anymore, and I reckon I've done my bit by showing you where that spot is. I'm going to keep moving for as long as I'm able, and see what else I can find."

I thanked him profusely, and that was the last time I saw him. But I definitely had plans for that little square of sunshine.

Chapter 2 – The Black Water

Finding the secret path to the little window into the sky reawakened the excitement and hope that I had been so alive with when I first entered the maze. This was finally something I could explore, something different and promising against the backdrop of monotony around me.

I slept for a while after saying goodbye to the old man, then headed directly back down the restricted tunnel. I found path my guide had showed me easily enough, and came to the pile of rocks in just a few minutes. It wasn't nearly as far as I had imagined when following the slow-going man with a limp.

I climbed up the pile of rocks, remembering where I had found the handholds, and was soon in position to gaze once more at the blue sky. But when I bent down and peered through the rocks, my heart skipped a beat as all I saw was darkness! What had happened to my square of sunshine!

"No...no, no, no, no, no," I moaned, sinking down and staring in disbelief between the two rocks. I stood up and looked around me, hoping I was mistaken about the location of the peek hole. But no, I had it right. I sank down again and just stared.

As my eyes adjusted, I realized that it was not completely dark however. There were little pinpricks of light. Then it hit me – stars! They were stars! I must have come to look out during the night! I never could tell what time it was in the maze, but here was a window into reality outside, and it was nighttime!

Once I realized the truth, I relaxed and reveled in the beauty of those stars. It was only a small patch, but it awakened the imagination inside of me. I dreamed of lying back on the ground, high in the mountains, and staring up at a whole sky of stars. I could almost feel the campfire behind me as my fantasy took shape. Why was it so hard to get there? What was this maze that was confounding my efforts, and how was I going to get out?

I soon turned my daily trips to the Sky Window into a thriving business. I started taking other people there so they could see the sunlight, or stars depending on their choice, in exchange for food, clothing, or anything else they had to offer. I would blindfold them for part of the journey to keep the path a secret. Nobody else ever saw the caution tape, which was the main marker for finding the path, so no one could ever come without me.

As I said, I would trade for just about anything people had to offer, but my favorite thing to receive was information. I started keep a notebook (which I had received from a young man as payment) of everything people could tell me about the maze. To be honest, I didn't learn very much really. Almost everybody just talked about miles and miles of concrete walls. There were stories of a real fruit tree somewhere – some people said it was apple and some said it was cherry – but nobody could really tell me how to get to it. Once, a mother with two kids in tow told me about a couple who would share food with those in need. It wasn't helpful information for me, but I felt sorry for her and took it as payment for the trip anyway. Her kids were astounded at the sight!

The more time I spent staring out at the sunlight the more I wanted to be out there, to feel its warmth on my face. When I was alone there, I started working on moving rocks so I could get closer to the little window. I was careful to work on the other side of the cave-in, so I wouldn't damage my peek hole. It was slow going, because I didn't want the rocks to shift and collapse.

"What if this was once the exit from the maze for everybody?" I wondered. What if this was the way out, only it had become blocked by an accident and everyone had forgotten about it? If I could clear a way out, I would be a hero! Think of what it would mean to go back and start leading people out of the maze for good!

Finally, I reached a point where I thought I could actually climb up next to the wall and reach the window! It was still above my head, but I could just get my fingers over the edge. All this time climbing and moving rocks had made me pretty strong, and even with my heavy pack I gingerly pulled myself up towards the ledge. I pushed forward and sprawled across the opening, sunlight washing over my face.

There was a half-second when I thought that I had made it, that I was free. Then I looked down, and down, and down, into the Abyss! I scrambled back from the edge, alarmed at the dizzying height, and then peered over carefully with dismay. There was no path, no stairs, no footholds, no anything except a straight drop into the Abyss below me! The mist rose up and I could smell the stench of death in my nostrils.

I can't even begin to describe the hopelessness and depression that overcame me at that moment. The promise of that patch of sunlight was just a lie. There was no way out.

There wasn't even the pleasure of being in the sunlight to be had with the stench of the Abyss rising up continuously.

I left the restricted tunnel that day and I never went back. I refused to take anyone else to see it or even show them where it was. It was all pointless. Why look at a glimpse of something you can never have? All of my work had really been for nothing. I felt like a failure.

I started walking again the next day. I didn't have a destination in mind, because I didn't believe there were really any destinations to be found. I was disillusioned and without hope. I think my backpack increased in weight by at least twenty-five pounds that day I had found out the truth. Now every day was the same. I would get up and I start walking, just walking. When I got too tired, I would sit or lie down and sleep. Then I would get up and do it again.

I had thought that I knew which way east was until I had climbed up to the window over the Abyss. By my calculations that should have been west, away from the fearful edge. I reoriented myself after discovering my mistake, and my guiding principle in walking was to do my best to leave that place of torment behind me.

And then one day I came across something new. I came around a bend that looked just like all the other bends and there was a pool of blackish water ahead of me. There were lots of people swimming and playing in it. It was the first time I had actually seen anybody who looked like they were having fun. But at the same time, the water was black and had a very distinctive odor, kind of like what was rising up from the Abyss.

Was there no way to put that awful place behind me for good? I turned to walk away when someone called over to me, "C'mon. Join us! It's great!"

This was also the first time anyone had invited me to do anything with them since I met the old man. All of the other people I had had dealings with had wanted me to show them that sunlight. I suddenly realized just how lonely I was. I hadn't really thought about it before, but I sure could have used some friends.

Still, that Black Water did not look very inviting. Did I really want to go out in that stuff? And then a thought occurred to me. If I were to wade out into that water – and I promised myself I wouldn't have to swim or dunk my head in, just wade out a little – then my backpack wouldn't seem so heavy. And if water was cool it would feel really good. Plus, I reasoned, it didn't seem to be hurting any of these other people. So, slowly, I waded out into the Black Water.

And it felt wonderful! It was cool and refreshing. I got used to the smell faster than I thought I would. And the best part was that I could hardly feel the weight of my pack at all. I could relax. I could lay back and float. It felt heavenly. As I lay there with my eyes closed, allowing my thoughts to get whisked away into oblivion, a boy splashed his way over to me. It was the boy that had invited me to swim.

"Hi, I'm Mark," he said as he stuck out his hand. He looked to be about my age, with dark hair that came down to his shoulders. He was dressed all in black, although that might have been because of the water. "You're new here, huh?"

I nodded.

"Yeah, that's what I thought," he said knowingly. "You can always spot the newbies. But I can tell you're already hooked, huh?"

"Hooked on what?" I asked, confused.

"The Black Water, Dummy!" he exclaims. "Most people who come here never leave. The water is so refreshing, there's nothing like it. And there are lots of great people here to hang out with. It's the easy life."

I had to admit that he might be right. Floating in that water did feel good, and it was a lot easier than walking and walking and walking. But I wasn't sure I was ready to give up my journey yet. Was there any chance of finding the way out of the maze?

"But what about discovering other places?" I asked. "What about the mountains or the Beautiful Valley? I still want to find them, if they exist."

"Oh, sure," Mark replied with a wave of his hand. "You can always go look for those places anytime. But most people that I know haven't ever found any of them. Most just end up back here, because there's nothing better."

As I pondered what Mark was telling me, though, things began to change! The water level of the pool started to go down! I look around as people started walking towards the edge, frustrated but not panicked. It only took a few minutes before the water was completely gone. I could then see that there was a drain at the bottom, and all the water had run down through it. I couldn't see what had caused it to drain, though. People all around me were groaning and complaining, and I looked over at Mark questioningly.

"Oh, yeah, that does happen sometimes," he answered my unspoken question. "It's a real bummer. But there's always another pool somewhere else, and everybody goes there.

Just then someone called out, "C'mon, I hear there is another pool just to the east of us!" And everybody started to run in that direction.

"See, what'd I tell you?" Mark cried triumphantly as he ran off with the rest of the crowd.

I stood there, uncertain. I had made it my mission not to go east, towards the Abyss. I wanted to go west, wherever that might take me. I remembered the Beautiful Valley. Was I ready to give up on it? Did I believe it was real? I needed for it to be real, because I needed to believe in something. There had to be a way to find it. So finally I made up my mind to continue my journey and started marching in the opposite direction from the other swimmers.

Only this time things were much, much worse, because now I was wet! All my clothes were wet with the Black Water. My backpack felt like it had gained a hundred pounds! And I was keenly aware that the stench was now on me. People that I passed seem to move away from me, to the other side of the path, although nobody said anything. My feet sloshed in my boots and I could immediately feel blisters forming. This was the worst experience of my life. I knew I would have to stop and let my clothes dry out. Why had I succumbed and waded into that water in the first place?

I decided to stop around the next corner, but when I made the turn there was another pool of Black Water! And once again there were lots of people playing in it! And there was Mark, waving at me with a big grin on his face. I knew that I needed to dry out, but maybe after one more swim, I thought, just to refresh myself. This time I jumped in headfirst and swam all around. It truly was an amazing feeling! But just like the last time, the pool started to drain after I had only been there a few minutes! Soon, the water was gone, and the other swimmers were too!

Once again I set out on my miserable trek. My head was wet and dripping and the smell was terrible. There was just nothing for it but to stop right there and get my clothes dried out. I leaned again the concrete wall and took off my boots, setting them over to one side. Then I stripped down to my undies and lay all my clothes out on the rock floor of the maze. For the first time ever I was grateful for how hot the maze felt all the time. I decided to go to sleep while I let my clothes dry out.

I don't know how long I slept – it seems like hours. I was so tired. When I woke up, though, I checked on my clothes and to my dismay discovered that they hadn't dried at all! In fact, they were still dripping! How could that be?

I felt I had no choice but to put the clothes back on. Grimacing, I slipped my feet back into the hiking boots with a squishing sound. I stood up and could see a pool of water forming at my feet where I stood. How could my clothes be this wet? Not knowing what else to do, I started walking, this time with a destination in mind. I was looking for another pool.

And it didn't take long until I found one. And there was Mark, splashing over to me as I swam out. "Where have you been?" he asked.

"I was trying to get dry," I replied.

"Oh, yeah, I forgot about that," he said with a shrug. "This water just kind of stays on you. But you don't notice it as long as you stay in the pool. Am I right?"

Only this pool dried up just like the others. This time I followed Mark pretty closely until we found another pool in just a matter of minutes. And another after that. And another after that. This pattern became my existence. I didn't even care whether I'm going east or south or west. I didn't care about a Beautiful Valley or forests or anything. I just needed to find the next pool. I really don't know how long I lived like that. Years probably.

Mark and I became good friends, always hanging out together. He introduced me to other people in the pools, but he and I became inseparable.

I would probably have done this for the rest of my life if not for what happened next. It was the single most pivotal day in my whole life when a man approached me, seemingly out of nowhere. He was dry and clean and energetic. Most people like that never came near the pools, and if we passed them in the maze looking for the next pool they always moved away from us and refused to make eye contact.

But this man was different for some reason. He walked right up to the edge of the pool where Mark and I were soaking. He said hello. He didn't seem to be bothered by our obvious smell or appearance. He looked us in the eye and talked to us with respect. He told us that he used to be just like us, and now he wanted to help us get out too, if we wanted to.

I knew immediately that I desperately wanted to leave this place, and just hadn't realized it until now. Life in the Pools of Black Water wasn't really life at all. I asked him if he could take us to the Beautiful Valley and he just looked confused. He said the only way out is to go to the mountains. That excited me. I asked him if it is east or west, because I didn't want to go east. I didn't admit that I hadn't paid attention to where I was going in a long time and didn't even know which way east was anymore.

Then he said something that shook me to the core. "Every path in the maze leads east. Every path leads to the edge of the Abyss. The only way to avoid it is to cross it. And there is only one bridge."

I was immediately excited, sure this man was our salvation. But Mark was decidedly less interested. "This guy doesn't know his left from his right," he complained. "It's all a bunch of mumbo jumbo that doesn't mean anything. Stick with the Black Water, am I right?" He looked intently at me, expecting me to agree. But I wasn't so sure. I wanted to believe this man, even though everything else I had seen told me I shouldn't get my hopes up again.

"Forget you then," Mark proclaimed, diving in and swimming away. I didn't want to make Mark mad, but there was something about what this man was saying that seemed right to me.

"So where is this bridge?" I asked.

"I will take you there," he replied enthusiastically. "Only it's not a there at all. It's a who."

I didn't really understand, but I promised to follow him. He reached out and put his hand on my shoulder. I thought with a start that nobody had touched me in a very long time. Even Mark, my best friend, was never physically affectionate. I was humbled that this clean, dry stranger would make contact with my disgusting, wet shoulder.

We set off. It was hard to keep up with the stranger in my wet clothes with my heavy backpack, while he was dry and had only a knapsack and a water bottle. As we hiked we passed several black pools that I want to stop at, but he wouldn't slow down. I looked out and thought I even saw Mark out in one of them, waving at me, but how could that be?

Finally, we came around a bend and I realized that we were outside of the maze! I never thought I would see real trees again! And overhead was real sky - beautiful, blue sky stretching out in all directions that made me laugh out loud to see it again. A little farther and I realized that we had come back to the path I had been on when I went into the maze! Had I really been that close to the entrance (or exit) the whole time?

We came back past the sign that read, "Find Your Own Way" and I thought with chagrin that I wasn't sure if I ever really did. I had thought that I was blazing my own path when I went up to the Sky Window, but that turned out to be a dead end. And swimming in the Black Water felt more like being trapped than it did being independent. Then we approached the edge of the Abyss again. Only this time there was someone else waiting at the edge. The man I had been following said that his name is Jesus, and he is the one who can take me across the canyon.

And then he left, and I was alone with Jesus.

-

Chapter 3 – The Bridge

Jesus stepped towards me like a figure stepping out of a blazing light. To be more accurate, it was as if a brilliant, blinding light was radiating from Jesus, and as he moved closer to me it somehow faded so that I could see him clearly before me. He looked commanding, but gentle; regal, yet kind. I have never seen anyone or anything like this before or since. It was as though Jesus was something totally different from the world, and yet totally comfortable and at home here at the same time. I felt as though I was in the presence of someone great, and that I should bow or prostrate myself or something, but I couldn't take my eyes off his face. He was smiling like he was excited to see an old friend, although I was sure we had never met before. I would have remembered!

This was not what I would have expected Jesus to be like. I mean, I honestly hadn't given Jesus much thought, but I had heard of him. I had heard he was a teacher, that he died and then came back to life, and even that he was God's son or something. That all sounded pretty amazing to me, and I thought of other stories about supernatural beings like Hercules or Superman. Someone like that should be tough and unyielding, superior to everyone else and ready to face down any evil in their midst.

So if someone like that had a Bridge that led over something like the Abyss, I would have thought they would be guarding it pretty carefully. They wouldn't want just anybody to go across it. They might demand payment, or some sort of proof that one was worthy. Quickly I began thinking through the things in my backpack, things that might make me a worthy candidate.

It seemed pretty obvious that I would not be able to bring up recent additions to my life. It was best to draw attention away from the Black Water and my time spent there. It was foolish to think that perhaps Jesus would somehow not notice, especially when I was obviously leaving a Black Water puddle wherever I stepped. Still, I could show Jesus some of the awards I had gotten as a kid. And I could definitely spotlight the time I had spent guiding people to the Sky Window. That was a definite highlight. And after all, I had never really hurt anybody. The Black Water looked bad, I had to admit to myself, but it didn't hurt anybody but me, did it? If seen in the right light, I was actually a pretty good person, I decided.

"What are we going to do to fix this?" Jesus asked as he drew close. His tone was kind and reassuring, not condescending at all.

"Um, Jesus. Hello," I blurted, not sure how to start. "So the man who brought me here – I guess he's a friend of yours – he said you could help me find some better direction in my life. You know, like a map or something, to get me through the maze."

"There is no way through the maze. It's a dead end. Haven't you figured that out by now? The only place it ever takes anybody is into the Abyss."

"Yeah, that's what your friend said too. So do you know another way that I could go?"

Jesus seemed amused at my question. "That depends entirely on where you want to go."

"If you know the way, I would really like to go to the mountains," I responded.

"I do know the way to the mountains. In fact, I am the way to the mountains," Jesus said cryptically.

"Oh good," I said, then barreled forward. "So let me show you what I've got. I'm really a good person, you know, so I have quite a bit to offer. For one thing, I know the path to the only Sky Window in the whole maze. That's what I call it – the Sky Window. It's a wonderful little window where you can see the blue sky even from within the maze. And I've taken lots of people to see it."

"Yes, I know," Jesus replied, still looking amused. "I also know that you climbed up to that window. Where did it lead?"

"Well, it overlooked the Abyss," I admitted reluctantly. "There's no where you can go. But the sky still looks amazing!"

"Kind of like the sky out here, away from the maze?" Jesus motioned upward and all around. There was no denying that the little Sky Window was pretty pitiful compared to standing under the real thing.

"Well, yes," I said, "This is better, of course. But I did the best I could with what I had. I helped lots of people find that Sky Window. And it helped them, gave them hope."

"For a small fee."

This wasn't going like I had hoped it would at all. "Well, I had to make a living," I said defensively. "But I didn't take from people who didn't have much to offer. I even let some people go for free because I felt sorry for them."

"OK, then let's see it."

I lowered my backpack off my shoulders and began rummaging through it. Finally, I pulled out a small figure representing my time at the Sky Window. I held it up, trying to ignore the Black Water stains and the water dripping from it down my hand and onto the ground between us.

Jesus sighed. He didn't say anything, and we just stood there for the longest time, with me holding the meager offering up between us.

Finally, Jesus repeated his earlier question, "What are we going to do to fix this?"

My heart filled with shame as I looked at the figure I was holding up, realizing that everything in my pack and even my very person all looked as ridiculously inadequate as it did. "I don't know," I answered meekly. "I don't know how to fix it. Nothing I do seems to make a difference."

"Now that's what I was hoping you would say," Jesus responded with a wink. Gently he took the figure out of my hands and put it back in my pack. I noticed that no Black Water clung to his hands even after he had touched it.

I was stunned and filled with relief that I had willingly admitted my failure, and even more stunned and relieved that he had accepted that answer. I realized that this was what he had been waiting for this whole time. He already knew the truth, somehow, as if he knew everything about me on the deepest level. Yet he still accepted me, talked with me, and even offered me hope.

"It's true that there is nothing you can do to help yourself," Jesus continued. "You are aware that the Black Water permeates everything about you. But even without the Black Water, the efforts made by you and others in the maze still do not get you very far. In fact, your best efforts are like staring at a little Sky Window and pretending like you are under the whole of the blue sky. Those performances that could be called the very best in the maze are still like a rag used to soak up Black Water. It's useless for you to come here and try to convince me of your worthiness.

"But that doesn't mean there is no hope. In fact, you can be assured that there is every hope that you will see the mountains very soon. That's because there is something I can do to fix you when you cannot fix yourself. Would you like to know what it is?"

"Of course!" I exclaim.

Jesus smiled. "This is both very simple and very profound. Let me explain to you what is really going on in this place that you have struggled so long to understand. Tell me, why do you want to get to the mountains so desperately?"

"There is just something about living in those mountains that has always drawn me," I said without hesitation. "It feels like they are calling to me, telling me that that is where I belong. But I don't know how to get there."

"You are drawn to the mountains because that is where you were created to be. You were created to be a hiker, a climber, a leaper, an explorer, and so much more. But the reason that you cannot get there is because of this Abyss. It goes all the way around the mountains, and it is too great for you to hike or climb or leap. It is too deadly for you to explore."

"But where did the chasm come from?" I asked, dismayed. "If I am meant to be in the mountains, why is it so hard to get there?"

Jesus smiled again. "But it's not hard to get there at all. Not anymore. All you have to do is come with me across my bridge. But I am getting ahead of myself. What was your question? Where did the chasm come from? Well, a long time ago, when everything was still new, the very first people put it there. You see, living in the mountains means living with my father, who made the mountains. But the very first people didn't want to do that. They wanted to live in the mountains but not with my father, and that just wouldn't work. So they left the mountains altogether. Their rebellion against my father was so devastating that it caused a great earthquake. And when the earthquake stopped, it had created this chasm. None of the people could get back across it to the mountains even if they wanted to."

Jesus continued, "My father also has an enemy, and that enemy saw that people would continue to try to get across the chasm and that they would realize they were wrong to rebel against my father. So he built the maze over here to distract people from the mountains. Most people forget all about the mountains and the chasm and live their whole lives in the maze caught up in its tricks and illusions."

"I'm so glad I didn't forget," I said, then caught myself. "Or at least, I didn't forget for long. "

"And yet you still carry the substance of the maze with you."

I realized that he was referring to the Black Water that was creating an ever-growing pool around my feet. I was so embarrassed, and again I was filled with shame. I had been a fool. There was no way Jesus would let me cross his bridge into the mountains like that. Surely I had ruined my only chance.

"I understand," I said. "Thank you anyway. I'm sorry I've wasted your time." And I turned to walk back towards the maze, feeling ashamed and pitiful.

"But you didn't let me finish the story," Jesus called after me, enticing me. "Don't you want to know what happens next? It's pretty good news, if you ask me."

I turned back, not sure where he was going with this. Was there something he could do with me even in this condition? Jesus had a huge smile on his face as he beckoned me back over to him.

"Here's the best part. My father loves you. He loves everyone. Even when the first people rebelled, he didn't stop loving them. In fact, right away he began drawing up plans to build this bridge. And he has sent me to spread the word that he isn't holding that rebellion against you or anybody else. He wants to be reconciled. He wants to invite everyone across this bridge back into the mountains with him."

"What's the catch?" I asked. This sounded too good to be true, like it might be some sort of sales pitch.

"It's not a catch," Jesus replied. "But I think you have already figured out that my father wants you, but he doesn't want the substance of the maze. In fact, he hates the substance of the maze because of how badly it hurts you. It's like a disease, like a cancer, destroying you from the inside out. And that's really what this bridge that I have built is. It is the one and only way to cure you from that cancer. If you try to get to the mountains without being cleaned up then you are doomed from the start.

He looked deeply into my eyes, his stare penetrating all my defenses. "Do you believe what I am telling you?"

I nodded, unable to look away and suddenly unsure of my voice. It sounded right, but at the same time I was really overwhelmed and not sure exactly what was going on.

Still holding my gaze, Jesus said, "I love you. Do you believe that?"

I've only just met him, but I was surer of him than I had been of anyone else in my entire life. I thought about it, and I decided that yes, absolutely, did I believe that Jesus loved me, in spite of what I had done to myself. Maybe it wasn't even that he loved me in spite of myself, but he loved me for who I am. But how could that be? There was no hiding everything about myself and I didn't even try, not anymore. Here was my backpack full of stuff. Here was my whole self, dripping with Black Water that never dries up.

"Yes," I said quietly but firmly.

"And do you want me to free you from your burdens?" he asked.

Again, I said "Yes."

"Then follow me," he replied. And with that he started walking toward the edge of the canyon. I followed, and this time I saw that there was indeed a bridge over the chasm. Was it here before, when I came by alone? How could I have missed it? Now I could see it stretching out before us as plain as day. And Jesus stepped onto this bridge, beckoning me to follow.

As we walked, Jesus continued to talk. "My father knows that if he directly attacks the substance of the maze while it is still in you that it will kill you too. That's the direct consequence of living in the maze. So my father and I came up with a plan to remove the substance from you and then destroy it."

"How do you do that?" I asked.

"I will take the substance of the maze into myself, and hold it while my father burns it up."

I stopped walking, just staring at Jesus. What was he talking about? Was he crazy?

Jesus turned back to me, an amused smile on his lips. "Actually, I've already done the work, when I built the bridge. I held the disease in my body, and my father eradicated it. Now all we are doing today is including you in that cleansing."

"But didn't that hurt you?" I asked, amazed.

"Yes," said Jesus with a hint of sorrow in his voice. "In fact, it killed me. But because it wasn't my sin, death couldn't hold me. My father raised me to life again."

I couldn't think of anything else I could say. I was dumbfounded that Jesus would do this for me, for everybody, even after we had rebelled against him.

We walked and we walked. The chasm below was bigger even than I had realized. Finally, we came to a place in the bridge where two paths led out away from the main bridge in either direction. Jesus led me onto one of these. After a few minutes, we came to the end. The bridge simply ended over the chasm. For a brief moment, I am afraid Jesus wanted me to jump into it! I guess that's what I deserved.

Instead Jesus turned to me, and he asked me to take off my backpack. I did, without hesitation. He opened it up and began lifting things out of it. Some of them I would never have shown to anyone, but with Jesus somehow I felt no shame. How could that be? When I had taken items out to show Jesus, I was filled with guilt and shame. But when I let him take them out, it was somehow OK. Even the best of the items that he pulled out were completely soaked in the Black Water. Some of the things Jesus removed he simply threw off the bridge! He simply chucked them into the abyss beneath us. And some of the things he wiped with his own white robes. Immediately, the Black Water was gone, and they were clean and beautiful. Yet Jesus' robes were not stained. Finally, the backpack was empty. There was a small pile of clean items next to Jesus.

Then Jesus turned to me again. "Strip," he commanded.

I was taken aback, but immediately began to obediently take off my disgusting clothes. Jesus took my wet, dripping clothes from me as they came off and turned to throw them over the edge. Finally I was standing there before Jesus, stark naked and still dripping with the Black Water. He told me to turn around, and there was a pool of pure, clean water behind me. I'm sure it wasn't here a minute ago.

"Bathe," Jesus commanded again. And I did. As I lowered my toes and then my whole foot into the clear water, I could see the blackness spread out from me, contaminating the water. I wondered if this water could wash enough of the Blackness away to make any difference, or if I would ruin it. Slowly I lowered my whole body into the water. Finally, I lowered my head into the water, and the difference was instantaneous. The water was warm and I realized that I had been shivering without even knowing it. I had thought the Black Water was refreshing in the hot, stuffy air of the maze, but now somehow it now seemed like it had been really ice cold in a freezing climate. This water was truly refreshing, warming me up to my very bones.

As I drew my head out of the water I looked back to see what Jesus was doing. To my surprise, he too had stripped and was stepping into the pool. At first the Blackness in the water seemed to move away from him, becoming more concentrated again around me. Jesus stopped about six feet away from me with his eyes still fixated on me. He smiled, then lifted his hands up, holding them outstretched as wide as he could. It was only then that I noticed the scars he had through both his wrists.

As if on cue, when Jesus raised his hands the Blackness in the water responded by flowing back towards him. In fact, it looked as though the Blackness were flowing into him! I looked down to see the Blackness being pulled off of me and onto him like he was magnet attracting iron shavings. On and on the Blackness went, leaving my body, flowing through the water between us, and being soaked into Jesus. I looked at Jesus' face. He was still watching me, still smiling, but there was pain in his eyes. What was I doing to him?

I couldn't believe how much Blackness came out of me. After what seemed like an eternity, the last of the Blackness left me and I was clean. The water returned to being crystal clear as all the Blackness disappeared into Jesus, and I couldn't see any remains of it on his body anywhere.

Jesus climbed back out of the pool and pulled his robes back on. "Stay as long as you like," he said his eyes now bright again. I still wasn't sure exactly what had happened, but I sank back into the warm water, just soaking in the purest, most satisfying water I have ever been in. I was aware that I was clean now for the first time since…ever.

"Why did you do that?" I said, breaking the silence. "Why would you take my Black Water like that?"

"I told you, I love you," Jesus answered. "This pool was created by my love for you, by the sacrifice of my life that I made for you.   My sacrifice created this Bridge so that you can cross and this Pool so that you can be cleansed."

I lay back, thinking about what Jesus was telling me. Most of it went right over my head.

"If your father eradicated all of the substance of the maze," I asked after a while, "then why is it still here?"

Jesus answered, "Because everyone has a choice. Just like the first people had a choice of whether to live with my father or not, so do you and everyone else. It's because of his love for you that he gives you the choice. Sadly, many people choose to live apart from my father and me. That separation is the essence of what the substance of the maze is."

Finally, Jesus beckoned me to come out and he wrapped a white robe around me. Then he wrapped me up in a giant bear hug. He was crying and smiling at the same time, and I was too. This was the perfect moment. I wished that it would go on forever and ever. But after what seemed like hours and yet only moments at the same time, he whispered in my ear, "I am so pleased with you." Then he turned and beckoned me to follow him back the way we came. I say follow, but really we walked side by side.

We came back to the center, and Jesus turned, leading me on across the rest of the bridge. As I looked back at the two arms reaching out from the center of the bridge, I realized that the bridge was shaped like a cross.

Finally, we reached the other side and stepped onto the grass once more. Rising up ahead of us was the mountains! They looked absolutely magnificent in the waning light of the setting sun. After moving a few hundred yards past the Abyss, we stopped and camped for the night. Jesus taught me how to build a campfire, and shared his food with me. As we ate, Jesus looked at me and said seriously, "You now live on the same side of the Abyss as I live. I am on your side. I washed your sin away in the pool and left it in the Abyss. We are now both on the same side of your sin, it is not between us. Do you understand?"

I nodded, but I'm not sure I did completely understand. In fact, I was sure that I did not.

Jesus continued, "There is still a road ahead of you, but you will never be alone, even when you do not see me. And nothing you do will ever come between us. Whatever it is, we will face it together.

"I don't know what you've heard about the mountains," he said, "but I want you to know that there will still be temptations there. There will still be people who don't understand that they are on the same side of the Abyss as I am. They think everyone has to be perfect now, and they look for ways to look like they are perfect. And they can be very judgmental of people who aren't perfect. I'm not looking for you to be perfect, only to be yourself. I am looking for you to get to know me better and to get to know my father better. But I know that there will be times when you make choices that are more like the maze than they are the mountains. Don't be discouraged. I'm not looking for you to grovel and tell me how pitiful you are and promise that you will stop sinning, stop swimming in black pools and do all the right things instead, because, as you say, there is nothing you can do that will make a difference. That kind of repentance is just part of a cycle that will lead right back to the same behavior and the same remorse and shame over and over again. The relationship that we now have is a gift that my Father gives you, an invitation to trust me by admitting you can't do anything and letting me do all the work instead. The intention not to sin is not the same as the power not to sin. You may try to give me your best intentions, but what I would rather do is give you my power."

Jesus reached into the folds of his robes and produced a water bottle, which he held out to me. "This water is my presence with you, all of the time. Even when you don't see me, you will know that I am with you. This water will strengthen you, guide you, and refresh you."

It looked just like the one carried by the man who had led me out of the maze, and I eagerly took it from Jesus and laid it down beside me.

Then Jesus lay down and went to sleep, and so I did the same.

Chapter 4 – The Path of Satisfying God

When I woke up the next morning, the sun was already high in the sky. I had been exhausted, I realized, and with good reason. The campfire had gone out, and I was alone, but there was a small pouch sitting on a rock that contained fruit, toast and bacon. It seemed that Jesus had gone. I sat and ate hungrily, anticipating the journey ahead of me into the mountains. Once I was finished I stood up and instinctively reached for my backpack, but it was nowhere to be found. Instead, next to me is a knapsack like the man who led me out of the maze had, and the water bottle Jesus had given me the night before. I drank deeply from it, and as I did I could almost feel the warm presence of Jesus with me again. I clipped the bottle to my belt and looked inside the knapsack. There were the things Jesus kept from my backpack, pure and clean now. I put it on, shocked that it had almost no weight at all. Then I turned towards the mountains and began to follow the trail before me. And though I could see the path rising before me, I did not feel the strain of walking uphill the way I had in the maze!

As I walked into the mountains and saw trees, real trees, beginning to surround me, I realized that Jesus had not given me the one thing that I had been hoping for most – a map! I had spent so much time in the maze trying to find one, or find someone with one, or even create my own, that it had become something of a fixation for me. Once I was out of the maze, the world seemed that much bigger. How would I find the right trails without a map to guide me? It just seemed like it was something Jesus should have provided. The most logical solution I could think of was that the path in front of me would be clearly marked by Jesus, giving me markers to follow as I walked. Perhaps there wouldn't even be choices to make, but just one straight path leading me forward.

But I didn't get very far before that notion was proven false. I came to a fork in the road, with one trail leading left and one trail leading right. Both continued up into the mountains. Thankfully, each path was identified with a sign, only they weren't as obvious as I was hoping. One said, "Satisfying God" with an arrow pointing off to the left. The other said, "Trusting God," with an arrow pointing to the path on the right.

"Now this is a conundrum," I thought to myself. They both seemed like the right path. I thought one would say something like "Followers of Jesus – This Way" while the other said something like, "Sinners – This Way". But both of these paths looked like trails Jesus would want me to be on. Was one better than the other? Jesus had invited me to trust him, so maybe that was the better path. But he had also said that he was pleased with me after I had bathed in the pool, after I had obeyed him. And surely he would want me to keep doing things that pleased him. That is what is meant by satisfying God, right? So I chose the left path – "Satisfying God."

I walked and walked, grateful that there were no more difficult decisions to be made. The farther I went, the more I began to see some other people on the path as well. Unlike the people in the maze, these people all had smiles on their faces and everyone said things like, "Hi! How are you? I am fine! Are you fine?" Everyone here is fine!" I felt reassured that I had chosen the right path because everyone else seemed to be doing well on it.

So I kept walking. After a couple of hours, I realized that my legs were getting tired. I could feel the incline of the path after all. I must have been mistaken earlier, because I was so relieved to be freed from that backpack. Still, I took pleasure in the burn in my calves, knowing that my walk was pleasing to God. Another swig from my water bottle revived me, although as I drank I got the distinct feeling that I was in the wrong place for some reason.

I came to another trail marker, although this one didn't identify a fork in the road. Instead, it said, "Please make a donation to help keep this path clean. God is pleased with a clean path." I dug in my pockets and found a few coins, so I tossed them into the bucket that was set up there, hearing them clink noisily as they hit the bottom. I wondered whose job it was to keep the path clean and why they needed money to do it. But it certainly looked like they were doing a good job, because there wasn't a stick or rock to be seen on the smooth path. I went on, forgetting about it quickly enough.

A little farther on, I came to a large shelf with rows and rows of hiking boots on it, marked a sign that said "No sandals allowed. Please wear only God-approved hiking boots." I thought this was strange because I was pretty sure Jesus was wearing sandals when I had met him the day before, but I could have been mistaken. I wasn't really looking at his feet. Acknowledging that whoever set this station up must know a lot more about Satisfying God than I do, I took off my own sandals and searched the shelves for a pair of boots in my size. I dropped my sandals into my knapsack and donned the heavy boots, glad to be satisfying God's will in my life.

The farther I went the more signs I saw, many of them visible before I had even passed the one before. Some were about wearing the right hiking gear, and I found myself adding more and more accessories to my outfit. Some were asking for more donations, but I had very little money and had put it all into the first bucket. Some told me to do certain things, like: "Stop on this spot and pray towards the mountain for five minutes," or "God is pleased if you help clear the path by picking up seven stones that others could trip over." I was certainly glad for the reminder to pray and took these opportunities to drink from the water bottle Jesus had given me, but I couldn't find any stones on the path so I just kept going. I had a nagging feeling that something was not quite right, but at the same time I felt confident in doing the things the signs told me to as often as I could. I decided that the uneasiness I was feeling must just be from doing things I was not used to doing, and being in a new place after all the time I had spent in the maze.

By the afternoon, I was starting to get tired of walking. It was a bright and sunny day, but by this time I was wearing heavy boots, a long-sleeved khaki shirt, khaki pants, a parka, and a wide-brimmed hat, all on top of the robes Jesus had given me, because that's what the signs had told me to do. And I felt like I was moving slowly because of so many things I have to do along the path. Frequent drinks from my water bottle did less to revive me than they had before. Still, if I was Satisfying God, then it was worth it, I reasoned. It was difficult going, but Jesus never said that it would be easy. And at least I had a purpose. When I thought about what life was like in the maze, I realized how much better it was now to be working for God's purpose in my life.

I came over a rise into a shady glen and decided to stop and rest. I moved off the path a little to sit on a fallen log. As I sat there, however, I smelled a familiar odor. It was one of those strange moments when you become acutely aware of what you smell, but don't want to believe it because it shouldn't be there. I began to investigate, moving away from the trail and searching behind bushes and trees. It wasn't hard to tell which direction the smell emanated from, and there, hidden in the tall grass, was a pool of Black Water! "Whoa!" I thought, "What is that doing here? And why would anyone get in that Black Water after they have already been cleansed by Jesus?"

Immediately I turned and walked quickly back toward the trail. I had no intention of spending any more time near that hideous pool than I had to, and I wished I hadn't even discovered that it was there. But I had discovered it, and my mind just would not leave it alone. I kept thinking about how hot and sweaty I was, and how good that pool always felt when I was in the maze. I pushed myself forward, moving down the trail at a brisk pace. I would leave that place far behind, and forget where it even was. Only my mind kept going back to that Black Water, and I could tell that even as I consciously tried to forget where it was, I was unconsciously memorizing the landmarks. There was the shady glen, the fallen log, and the long grass. And then I began to wonder if the water would even be the same out here in the open air. My clothes would probably even dry out here in this sunshine, I reasoned. The mountains air was totally different from that dank concrete maze.

And before I could even comprehend what I was doing, I had turned around and gone back down the path, found the glen, turned at the log and jumped headfirst into the Black Water. And it did feel just as good as I remembered it. Only, I felt guilt at the same time. "Why am I so weak?" I thought to myself. "I'm so ashamed. I've ruined the robes that Jesus gave me. What am I going to do?"

I crawled out of the water, looking around to make sure nobody saw me. Just as I had feared, my khakis were black and dripping. Then I opened up my shirt to look at the robes underneath. I was amazed to see that the robes were still white after all! Everything I had gathered along the trail was black and ruined, but the robes Jesus gave me were clean. I could still feel the wetness against my skin, even though the robes were dry.

"I don't deserve to have been freed from the maze", I thought. "I don't deserve Jesus' forgiveness or cleansing. I don't deserve to be on this path called 'Satisfying God' at all, because of what I just did. God could not possibly be satisfied with me after that. What would Jesus whisper in my ear now?"

I started to take a drink from my water bottle, but decided against it. I didn't deserve for Jesus' gift to make me feel better. But maybe, if I worked even harder and obeyed all the signs, I could make it up to him. And with that, I bent down and picked up several rocks from beside the black pool and stuffed them into my knapsack. It was heavier now, and that's exactly what I needed.

I thought about removing the disgusting khakis and going on in just the white robes Jesus had given me, but decided against it. Anyone I met would wonder why I had not obeyed all of the signs. Was it better to look like I had been Satisfying God but somehow gotten dirty, or to look like I was disobeying God but stayed clean? I decided to former would invite less questions.

I waited in the glen until the sun went down, wanting to avoid other people on the trail. Even hours later, my khakis were still dripping. Finally, when I was convinced that I would be alone, I continued up the path. Just a few hundred yards of hiking and I discovered the way ahead was up a long flight of steps carved into the side of the mountain. There was a sign that read, "Stairs of Repentance" and claimed there were 777 steps.

"Perfect," I thought to myself. This was exactly what I needed to show Jesus that I wouldn't mess up again. With that resolve, I began to trudge up those steps with purpose and commitment in my heart.

It was a long, hard climb. I don't know if there really were 777 steps or not, but it felt like a million. The extra weight that I had added to my knapsack certainly took its toll, but it also felt familiar. When I eventually reached the top, I was feeling exhausted but much better about myself. Surely such a punishment would make up for my earlier mistake.

I set up camp for the rest of the night. Sunrise was only a few hours away, and I was ready for sleep. I started a campfire the way Jesus had taught me, hoping it would help dry out my clothes.

The next morning, I was encouraged to see that my khakis had dried out some. They were still damp and still obviously blackened and stained, but at least they weren't leaving puddles wherever I walked. I hadn't been able to see it in the dark, but ahead of me was a large, ornate building. Giant, stone pillars rose high into the sky every ten or twelve feet, encircling white marble walls covered with intricate carvings of swirls and loops. Two huge, wooden doors stood out ominously against the white building. As I approached cautiously, I could read the sign over the door saying, "Hall of Good Works." That sounded promising.

The doors were shut, but unlocked. I peeked my head in, wondering if I should have knocked, and saw before me a huge foyer with vaulted ceilings and marble tile floors. I stepped quietly inside, grateful that I was no longer dripping but painfully aware of how dirty I must look. In the center of the otherwise empty room was a receptionist's desk, with a single individual sitting behind it. I made my way up to the desk to find an older man with a big smile on his face sitting there, staring at me as though waiting for me to make the first move.

"Hi! How are you?" I asked rather timidly.

"Oh, I'm fine," he replied, still sporting the huge smile. "How are you?"

"Pretty tired. Those were a lot of steps, and I only got a few hours of sleep last night."

"But you are fine, right?" he asked with a sharp look.

"Oh, yes, I suppose I am," I answered, a little taken aback.

"Then why aren't you smiling?" I stood frozen, not sure how to respond. The man impatiently motioned to a bucket beside him. The bucket was full of masks.

It was only then that I took a good look at the man's face and realized that he was wearing a mask. The big smile I saw as I came up was part of that mask, and it remained throughout our conversation. His eyes behind the mask revealed a tiredness or sadness that I could not explain. The bucket that he motioned to was full of masks identical to the one he was wearing. Slowly, I reached in and picked one up. The man was still watching me, expectantly. I slid the rubber band over my head and the mask slipped down over my own face.

With this, the man was satisfied. He looked me over, seeming to just then realize what a mess I was. He didn't say anything about it though, for which I was grateful, instead informing me where I could buy some new hiking gear and clothes. With a start I realized that I didn't have any money left after giving the donations along the trail, but the man told me that I could buy on credit. I would be given chores to do in the Hall in order to pay it off. Then he assigned me a room to stay in and an itinerary of activities to do that he said were designed to Satisfy God. Then he handed me a map of the complex.

I followed his map through a network of hallways, passing many closed doors and going through several open atriums with glass ceilings to allow people to see the blue sky above. Everything was immaculate and clean. People walked everywhere, busily going from place to place. All of them wore the same smiling mask. It seemed a little creepy, I thought to myself.

The map led me right to the room that I had been assigned without incident. I noted with satisfaction that this was the first map I had received since my journeys began, and it was just as helpful as I had always believed it would be. My room was small and simply furnished, but comfortable. It had been a long time since I had slept in a bed. There was a binder on a small desk full of descriptions of the amenities available, the activities going on, and plans to gain bigger and nicer quarters through exemplary service to the Hall and to God. There was even a small refrigerator with a specially designed slot for my water bottle. I didn't really have anything to do to get settled, so I again followed the map down to the store where I was fitted with new khakis and gear. I was supplied with two pairs of hiking boots, one for indoors and one in case I ever needed to go outdoors. Strange, I thought, that we would wear hiking boots inside, and stranger still that I was expected to go outside only if necessary.

The next morning I started down my list of assignments. There were times of exercise, times of prayer, chores to do, classes with other masked people who all insisted they were "fine", and so forth. It wasn't long before I had settled into a routine, and hardly ever needed the map to guide me through the complex network of hallways anymore.

One of the classes that I took was called, "Cleaning Up." It was all about getting rid of sin and living a righteous life. There were lots of people in this class, more than any of my other classes by far. But the funny thing was that nobody in the class ever admitted to struggling with any particular sins. People talked about struggling, or overcoming, or putting sin behind them, but they always used generic terms. And nobody ever confessed to recent struggles or failures. The leaders of the class talked a lot about honesty and accountability, with everyone nodding and agreeing, but nobody ever really did it. Once, on one of my first days in the Hall, I started to bring up the Black Water, but the leader quickly silenced me, telling that we didn't want to talk about things that might make others uncomfortable. Someone else pointed out that there were children in the room. Then the person sitting next to me patted me on the back and said emphatically, "Thank God he's saved us from all that, right?" I decided not to speak up in that class anymore.

Still, as I got into the rhythm of the Hall I felt comfortable and satisfied. I settled in for the foreseeable future. Sometimes I wondered about the path outside – after all we were nowhere near the summit of the mountain and we certainly weren't getting any closer when we never even went outside, but I reassured myself that I was doing what I was told and therefore was satisfying God. That's really what Jesus wanted from me, wasn't it?

As time went on, though, I began to get more and more frustrated. I was doing all of the right things, but I didn't feel like I was getting any closer to God. I didn't feel like I was getting anywhere. The longer I was there, the more the Hall of Good Works seemed fake, and all the people seemed fake too. Why were we wearing masks? Why did we always have to be "fine"? One evening as I was brooding in my room, I pulled out the map I had received when I had first arrived. Looking at the complex pattern of hallways and corridors reminded me a lot of a maze. Why hadn't I noticed that before?

My growing frustration eventually led to depression. I denied it of course, faithfully wearing the mask whenever I was outside of my room. But then one day, my prayer manager embarrassed me in front of everyone because I messed up on one of the recitations. He laughed at me in front of everyone and told them the mistaken words I had used instead. It reminded me of the boy who made fun of my journal entry when I was young. I felt like the walls were closing in around me, and for the first time I was glad I had the mask to hide behind. But as soon as class was over, I hurried to my room and shut the door, ripping the mask off and gasping for air.

I felt like I was going to scream, and maybe start throwing things. But I knew that wouldn't be tolerated very well by the managers. I needed something to help me feel better, to calm the storm that was growing in my mind. So I made a decision. I decided to go back down the steps to the Black Pool. My plans just seemed to make themselves. I would do it in the dark, and be back in my room by morning. I had enough money by then to buy a second set of hiking clothes that I could hide outside and change before coming back into the Hall. Nobody would know the difference. If there was anything the people here were exceptional at, it was not noticing things.

The first night I carried out my plan, I was shaking as I made my way out through the double doors. Nobody said anything though, and I quickly switched to my outside boots. It had been several months since I been down this path, but I found the pool without any trouble. I took off the mask I had been wearing all that time in the Hall, and felt immediate relief that I was away from that place. I slid into the dark water and relaxed. It felt so good. After a time, I climbed out of the water, changed into my dry khakis, and hid my wet ones in the hollow end of the fallen log. I climbed back up the Stairs of Repentance, taking time to focus my thoughts so that I really meant it, and then silently slipped back into the Hall and up to my room. I had been right that nobody noticed at all.

That night started a pattern in my life that went on for some time. I would go down to the Black Water night after night, whenever I needed to, but still worked to please God in the daytime. Some nights I felt horribly guilty, and would cry and beat myself on my way back up the Stairs of Repentance. Some nights my shame doesn't faze me at all, and I race up the steps two at a time.

One night I came up out of the water just as I always did and headed back towards the log in order to change my clothes. I was shocked to realize that there was somebody sitting on the log already. It was Jesus.

Immediately, I was filled with shame and remorse. To be honest, I was more afraid of what he might do to me than anything else. I wanted to hide. Maybe I could sneak back into the grass and get back to the path without him seeing me. I would have to climb back up to the Hall of Good Works in my stained and wet khakis, but what alternative did I have? If I could just get back, I would never go down there again, I told myself.

I started wondering what Jesus was doing there in the first place. Why couldn't Jesus have come during the day, to the Hall, and seen me working diligently to please him? Why did he have to come to that spot at that time on that night?

Then he called my name. Of course he knew I was there. There was no sneaking away or hiding from him. Quickly, I put my mask back on and came out to stand before him, dripping and full of shame.

"What are you doing?" he asked. He sounded serious, but not necessarily angry. I tried to explain about the pressures of satisfying him, about how I just needed some relief, and that I could see how wrong it was for me to come here, so I would never do it again, that I was really sorry, and would work harder to make it up to him, by carry more rocks up the Steps of Repentance, and whatever else he wanted me to do…

Jesus let me speak until I ran out of things to say. When I was finally quiet, he said simply, "Why didn't you trust me?"

I looked blankly at him. "What?"

Again, he said simply, "Why didn't you trust me? I told you that I love you. I told you that I was the only one who could save you from yourself. I told you that we would face your sin together, on the same side. But now you are trying to hide it from me and even justify it. That doesn't work. I can see right through all of your pretenses."

I felt despair overcoming me as the truth of his words sank home. There was nothing I could say besides, "I'm sorry," and those words seemed painfully inadequate.

Jesus continued, "Why do you think my desire for you is to free you from the Black Water?"

I realized that I hadn't really thought about it like that. "Because…" I mumbled, "Because it's bad for me." It was half statement, half question.

"That's true," Jesus replied patiently, "But there is more to it than that. I love you, and so I want what is best for you. I know even better than you do that the Black Water is hurting you, destroying who I have created you to be. The more you choose it over the path I have designed for you, the less serious it will seem to you but the more damage it will do to you. Fundamentally, the Black Water is the opposite of the life I have given everything for you to live. When you choose it over me, you are in essence saying that the life I have given you isn't good enough for you. I say that we are on the same side of your sin together, and you are saying that you would rather be on one side with your sin while I am on the other side."

What followed was a blur of crying and repenting and hugging and more crying. When I saw my actions through Jesus' eyes, I understood the truth of how I had been defying him. It just made it worse to think that I was trying to make it up to him through each day working in the Hall of Good Works. It just made me a hypocrite. A change happened in my heart that night, as I really felt loved by Jesus, loved enough that he would confront me when I was hurting him and bringing harm to myself.

Finally, Jesus drew back and said, "There is more that I need to talk to you about. I didn't come here tonight simply because you went swimming in the Black Water. I came here because you have been on a harmful path for a long time. For some time now, you have trying very hard to manage your sin and your righteousness on your own."

"I don't understand." I replied. I thought I had been doing everything right until my failure sneaking down to the Black Pool.

Jesus continued, "I know the Hall of Good Works is attractive. But it isn't what I want for you. Instead, it is really based upon a lie. The Hall of Good Works is based upon the belief that if you do more of the right things and less of the wrong things, then that equals righteousness."

"And isn't that true?" I asked quizzically.

"Far from it," Jesus said sadly. "That completely disregards the righteousness that I already gave you. Look down at yourself. Where is the robe that I put on you when we were on the Bridge together?"

It was still under my hiking gear. I opened my jacket to reveal it.

Jesus said, "See, I put my righteousness on you. Why would you want to cover it up with all this other stuff, with your attempts at your own righteousness? And look, the Black Water ruined all of your clothes, but the clothes I gave you are still as white as snow."

It was true, and the whole truth hit me like a ton of bricks. I had been failing to trust Jesus every since I chose the path of "Satisfying God" over the path of "Trusting God". I thought I had been trusting God all along while doing the tasks in the Hall, but really I had been relying only on myself. When we were on the bridge, I trusted Jesus with everything because I could do nothing myself. And that was what pleased him. But my efforts to please him without trusting him were worthless from the very first step.

"I understand," I said. "I cannot do this on my own. I cannot stop doing wrong. I cannot start doing right. I need you to do it for me."

And once again Jesus hugged me. He helped me take off the wet clothes that had been covering my robes. He helped me take the rocks out of my knapsack. Then he turned with a laugh and added, "And take off that silly mask."

I slipped it off rather sheepishly and dropped it on the pile of wet khakis.

"And where is the water bottle I gave you?" Jesus inquired. "I believe it would have helped you see the truth of your situation a long time ago, if you had been drinking from it and paying attention."

I had almost forgotten all about it. It sat snugly in its place inside my refrigerator back in the Hall of Good Works.

"I don't want you to go back, even to retrieve it," Jesus said. "Take your wet clothes and go throw them into the Black Water where they belong. Do the same thing with the dry ones that are in this log, come to think of it. I will be back momentarily."

Jesus slipped between the trees and was gone almost before his words could register in my mind. I gathered up all of the supplies he had mentioned and carried them back down to the water. I threw them in and watched them sink. When I returned to the log, Jesus was waiting for me with my water bottle in hand. "Don't leave it behind again," he said sternly.

Then he led me back down the path away from the Hall of Good Works, away from the Steps of Repentance, to the fork in the path and to the one marked "Trusting God."

Chapter 5 – The Path of Trusting God

In many ways, just being on the Path of Trusting God was exhilarating. For one thing, I felt alive. I mean, really alive! I walked along, enjoying the feeling of the crisp air on my face and the smell of the forest in my nostrils. I was excited to see what was around every bend and over every rise. I felt like I was somehow connected to the rocks and trees and wildlife around me, and everything seemed sharper, more in focus, more real than it ever had before. I found myself dreaming about the future, more hopeful than I had been in a long time. When I was in the Hall of Good Works, everyday was the same and it never felt like we got anywhere, something it had in common with the maze. Now I was free to hike and climb and explore and rest and swim and whatever else I found to do.

You see, this trail didn't have a Hall. There was no building I was supposed to stop and live in. There was no itinerary I was supposed to follow, and no managers keeping me accountable for doing the job right. It was very freeing, to be sure, but also frightening. I found myself pondering the ramifications of such a bold truth. "If I'm free," I thought, "then aren't I more likely to make the wrong choice? Haven't I been making wrong choices all my life? How could lifting the restraints help me to be a better person?"

As excited as I felt to be traveling this trail, I was also deeply aware of how vulnerable and exposed I felt. I was acutely aware that I wasn't wearing the mask anymore – I dropped it into the Pool of Black Water where Jesus helped me take it off. And though many times before I had longed to leave it behind, now I found myself continually reaching for it in short bursts of panic, especially when I passed someone else on the trail. I was keenly aware that this was the real me – that anyone looking, friend or not, could see me for who I am. In some ways this seemed profoundly right – "I am a child of God, a friend and sibling of Jesus. I am loved by Jesus just the way that I am. What do I have to be ashamed of?" But at the same time it was very disconcerting. I knew there were plenty of people who would not be so easily impressed. I knew plenty of people who would be quick to point out that I still needed to be fixed in a lot of ways, and was sure it was better to hide my imperfections than advertise them.

And that's the question that really plagued my mind, over and over. "Am I really fixed?" I would ask myself. "Do these white robes I wear – the ones that Jesus put on me – really mean that I am righteous? I certainly haven't done anything to give evidence of that. I've gone swimming now in the Black Water more than once while wearing these robes. And even when I was in the Hall of Good Works, I didn't feel like I was doing that well at the chores they gave for me to do. Jesus had said that I was a new creation and that I was made righteous in him. The big question I posed to myself was, "Do I really believe him? Do I trust what he says over my own perception and experience? Can believing what Jesus says about who I am do more to transform me than working on my sin the way I tried to do on the Path of Pleasing God?"

One day I came over a little rise to see a small waterfall coming down the side of the mountain into a little pool of refreshing, clear water with a stream winding away into the distance. I stopped and washed my face, enjoying the refreshing sting of the cold mountain water. As I dipped my hands into the water, I saw dozens of tiny tadpoles scattering in all directions. I reflected on how amazing it was that they could be so still that I hadn't even seen them until they moved. I wondered how they had even gotten to this mountain stream in the first place, and hoped their presence didn't mean the croaking of bullfrogs all through the night!

As I watched the tadpoles, however, I also noticed that the bottom and area around the pool was not ordinary mud, but clay. I picked some up in my hand and realized that it was just the right consistency to be shaped and molded without dissolving.

I'm not really an "artsy" person. I never have been. I enjoy art, but I've never quite gotten the hang of creating anything good. That didn't stop me from forming a beautiful sculpture in my mind, though. As I squished my fingers through the clay in the pool, I began to picture a perfect model of Jesus giving me a giant bear hug, the way that he did on the bridge and again when we left the Pool of Black Water. In my imagination, it was already fully formed and I couldn't wait to show it to Jesus the next time I saw him.

So after only a little hesitation, I got started. "Sorry, little tadpoles," I said out loud as I scooped up handfuls of clay and carried them a few feet away, to a flat rock that I could use as a base for my creation. Carefully, I began to mold the shape upwards, trying to represent two people in an embrace. It was rough going because I didn't really have any experience with this, but I pressed on, spurred by the excitement of my vision. I spent the whole afternoon on it, and finally had the general shape of what I wanted. I decided to wait until the next day to begin on the detail work.

With a few hours left before dark, I decided to go for another hike. I would return to make camp next to the pool. So I made my way upward, to see if I could find out where the little waterfall was coming from.

It was a steeper climb than I expected, and I had to stop to catch my breath several times. I was definitely off the beaten path, as the saying goes. That's why I was so surprised to find someone else up there. As I rounded the top of the hill to find an open area, there was a rustle in the bushes that I expected to be an animal, but it turned out to be a young man.

"Hello," I said, announcing my presence.

He seemed as surprised to see me as I was to see him. It looked like he had made camp up there and had been there quite a while. He had a tent, a fire pit, a folding chair, and even a clothesline strung between two trees. But what really caught me off guard was that he was wearing a mask – the kind handed out by the good people of the Hall of Good Works. But if I surprised him, I thought, then that meant he'd been wearing that mask even when there wasn't anybody else around.

"Hello," he answered. "What are you doing here?" he sounded friendly enough, but wary.

"I'm just out for a hike," I responded. "Do you live up here?"

"No," he said a little too quickly. "No, I live down on the Path. I just come up here to get away from the stress of everything, you know."

I told him that I was new to the Path of Trusting God, and asked what stresses he had found on this trail.

"Oh, well, you know," he answered. "People are always expecting you to 'get it' – you know, the whole being a new creation and living loved by God thing. But I'm not sure I always do, so I have to fake it just like I did on the other Path."

I was close enough now to see his mask clearly, and realized he had altered it. It was clearly one of the smiley-faced masks from the Hall of Good Works, but he had painted it with bright colors and taped a halo onto it. It looked rather silly to me, but I didn't say anything.

I wasn't sure what to think about what he had just said either. I hadn't met very many people on the Path of Trusting God yet, but I already had the impression that they were different - more accepting, more relaxed. I certainly didn't feel like I really understood what Jesus was talking about yet either. I began to wonder if this young man was describing something true, something I just hadn't realized yet. Were people on this Path going to put expectations on me to live this out the same way they did in the Hall of Good Works?

"So why are you still wearing a mask?" I asked finally. "Jesus told me to take mine off."

"Oh, yeah, sure," he said with the wave of his hand. "And I plan on taking it off just as soon as I'm really living up to it, you know. The mask just helps me feel more comfortable until I find the right way to do that."

"What do you mean by the right way?"

"Oh, you know, the right technique. The right plan. I know I'm not fixed yet. I know I can't keep up with those guys in the Hall of Good Works. But there's something about this whole grace technique that I just haven't figured out yet either. There's something still missing from the equation. I need a paradigm shift. So I come up here and I keep wearing the mask until I figure it out, you know."

"I don't really think that's how it works," I say slowly, thinking through what I wanted to say carefully. "I'm certainly no expert, but it seems like you're still living like you're on the Path of Satisfying God, only using different vocabulary and looking for different Good Works than they have in the Hall."

I tried to be gentle, but my words still stung, apparently. The young man started to cry, tears running down from behind the smiling mask. If it wasn't so tragic, it would have been comical.

"You're right," he blubbered. "You're right. What's wrong with me? I just can't get it right. Everybody else seems to have this grace thing figured out, and I just can't get it, no matter what I do. Everybody else moves on up the Path and I just stay here."

I found myself really wishing there was someone else there, someone with better answers than me. I certainly did not feel equipped to address this man's struggles. But I did the best I could, taking a drink from my water bottle then pressing on. I could hear the words I was saying being spoken to me and my circumstances at the same time as I said them to the young man.

"I think perhaps you are trying too hard," I said reassuringly. "I don't remember Jesus saying anything about figuring something out for ourselves, and I don't think grace is a thing to be manipulated or used. I think you would do well to just be you. I think that's who Jesus loves, and I think he wants you to love you too. I think if you could accept who you are and stop trying to be who you think you're supposed to be, then you would be a lot happier."

"That's it!" he exclaimed suddenly, jumping up. "That's what I've been looking for! That's the strategy I've been missing! I need to take steps to accept myself for who I am. Thanks."

With that, he started taking down his tent and gathering his stuff. But it seemed to me like he just took my words and used them for exactly what I was trying to speak against. I figured I really wasn't the one to talk to people, and hoped I hadn't done more harm than good. He broke camp with just excitement that in just a few minutes he was racing back down the mountain toward the trail. I noticed he was still wearing the mask.

I was frustrated as I made my own way back down the mountain. What could I have said differently to have helped him? I kept replaying the conversation in my mind. What else could I have said or done? And did I really believe the things that I had said, about accepting who I am and just being me because that's who Jesus loves?

I stopped to take another big swig from my water bottle. Remarkably, it never ran out of water! And it usually helped me focus on Jesus and the things that he had showed me. "Yes", I thought. "I do trust Jesus and the words that he spoke. I am a new creation. I am loved by God."

I made my way back to the clear pool and my unfinished sculpture and set up my own camp for the night. It was nothing as elaborate as what the young man had – just a sleeping bag on the ground and a hastily created fire pit. I had a tarp in my pack in case of rain, but looking up at the bright stars above me suggested it would be a clear night, and I loved to look up at the night sky.

When I woke up the next morning, I immediately got back to work on my sculpture. I worked on the image of my own face for a long time, reminding myself to be patient because I really wasn't very good at this sort of thing. Admittedly, it didn't really look very much like me, but at least it looked somewhat realistic. Slowly I formed my clay face so that it showed joy and surrender at the same time. Or at least I thought it did. I couldn't decide if the eyes should be open or shut, and how big the smile should be. After what seemed like hours, I decided I had something I could live with.

So I turned to working on the sculpture of Jesus' face, but quickly found myself struggling with a real conundrum. When Jesus gave me that hug, I certainly couldn't see his face. Was he smiling? Was he crying? Were his eyes open or closed? I soon gave up and decided to get back to it the next day. "The afternoon is for exploring," I said to myself.

Since I had climbed up the hill where the waterfall came from the day before, I decided to try the other direction this time, down the Path a ways and up into the hills to my left. Again, I came across someone else along the trail. This time it was a girl, and she was kneeling next to a large rock, crying.

"Hello," I called out as I approached, feeling awkward about her obvious distress.

Quickly she turned away from me and picked something up off the ground. I realized it is another mask as she slipped it over her head before turning back in my direction and leaning against the rock.

"Hello," she answered weakly.

"Are you OK?" I asked, moving a little closer. I stopped when she was about ten feet away.

"Oh, yes, I'm fine," she replied, but her voice was shaky and she kept her head down. She seemed nervous. Was she afraid of me, or just anxious about whatever was causing her to cry?

I moved closer still, finally sitting down next to her. I waited, not sure what to say. After a while, she glanced up at me. "Where's your mask?" she asked.

"I don't wear it anymore," I said. "Not since Jesus helped me take it off and start on the Path of Trusting Him."

She looked startled, and scrambled to her feet. "Oh, I've heard stories about that Path. People who talk about loving Jesus, but they don't do the work of pleasing him. I've heard they sin all the time and use grace and trust as excuses for not repenting." Her voice grew stronger as she expressed her convictions.

I was more surprised by her words than her animosity, however. "Aren't you on the Path to Trusting God?" I asked, taken aback.

"No way!" she exclaimed, taking three steps back. "I'm a true believer! I came from the Hall of Good Works right over there." She pointed behind her, and it was only then that I realized an important point. The trip I took down one Path and up the other was long, but there turned out to be more direct shortcuts cut across between them. I imagined that the farther up the Path I went, the less true that would be. But early on, I realized with a start, I could be back in the Hall of Good Works in just a few minutes. As I oriented myself with this new information, I also realized how close the Pool of Black Water must be. I had thought I had put it far enough behind me that it wouldn't be a temptation anymore.

My attention quickly turned back to the girl, however. I hadn't talked openly with anyone who was committed to the Path of Satisfying God since I left, and it hadn't dawned on me that some people might not welcome the change as much as I did. She was getting more and more belligerent as she talked about "those people" who live on the Path of Trusting God. It seemed clear it me that her diatribe was rehearsed and not from personal experience.

"Wait," I said, interrupting her. "What you are describing it the exact opposite from what I have experienced. When I was in the Hall of Good Works, I actually had a stronger desire to sin than I do on the Path of Trusting God. I know it sounds turned around, but the more pressure I felt to do the right things all the time, the more I wanted to do the wrong things."

"Like what?" she asked. "There aren't any wrong things to do in the Hall. It's all kept pure."

I wasn't any more prepared for this than I was the conversation with the young man the day before, but I pressed on anyway. "I like to swim in the Black Water Pools," I admitted, speaking quickly. "Or rather, I desire to swim in them. I can't say I really like it, because it always leads to shame and self-loathing. But when I lived in the Hall, I would sneak back down to a Pool and go swimming at night."

But she didn't hear anything after the words "Black Water Pools". She was pointing her finger right at my face, practically yelling at me, "See, that's what I'm talking about. You spend your time doing 'that' and use grace as an excuse to say it's OK."

"No, that's not what I'm saying at all," I argued futilely. "I'm saying that when I was on the Path of Good Works, I was more likely to give in and go down to the Black Water. Now I'm learning that Jesus can fill that need. It's not about saying 'no' because I'm not strong enough to do that, and the longer I succeed the stronger the desire. Now it's about letting Jesus show me how that desire isn't really meeting my needs after all."

But I might as well have been talking to the trees. Still pointing a finger at me, she began to back away in the direction of the Hall. I never did find out why she was out there crying by herself.

I was still sitting next on the rock where she had been kneeling. I felt awful. I had thought that if I had the strength to share my sinful struggle, that people would be accepting and maybe even open up about their own pain. But it hadn't worked like that at all. She had thrown my words back in my face. She had used it against me, to make her own point. I had thought that I could convince her that my path was better, but instead I had reinforced her negative convictions.

As I started to push myself up off the rock, I saw something half-hidden by leaves where the girl had been sitting. In her hurry, she had left it behind. It is a water bottle like mine, but wrapped up with brown paper. I assumed it must be a way to decorate things the way young girls like to do, and was wondering if there was a way I could return it to her when I heard voices from the direction of the Hall of Good Works.

"Right over here," I could hear the girl saying. Then she marched through the trees with three men following her, all walking intently towards me. They stopped about ten feet away.

"What are you doing out here?" one of the man demanded. "What do you want with my daughter?"

"I don't mean anybody any harm," I said franticly, alarms going off in my head. This could go very badly very quickly. "I was just talking with...your daughter. I found her out here."

"That's a lie, Daddy," the girl said matter-of-factly. "I would never come this far from the Hall, but I was tricked." She turned to point a finger at me, shouting," Why were you talking about Black Water to me?"

With a shock I realized I might be in real trouble. It was her word against mine, which was an argument I was sure to lose, and anyway, I had no desire for any kind of confrontation. "Now hang on..." I started, but the man was coming towards me.

"What's that in your hands?" he asks.

I looked down, remembering that I was holding the girl's water bottle. I held it out, "Oh, yes, she left this here. I was just trying to figure out how to get it back to her."

"I've never seen that bottle in my life, Daddy," the girl insisted. "My water bottle is right here." She held up another bottle of clear, pure water.

The man was close to me now, too close for my comfort. He reached out and tore the brown paper away from the bottle in my hands. Inside the water was black! What was that girl doing with Black Water? And what was she trying to do to me now?

Something hard glanced off the side of my head, and I saw stars. I spun to my left and registered that the other two men had picked up several stones each. One of them let a second stone fly, and it whizzed past my ear. Without a thought, I turned and started running back into the trees.

I could hear the girl's father yelling at me as I ran. "Don't let me catch you and your Black Water around my daughter again, or you'll be sorry!" It sounded like that meant he wasn't going to chase me, but I wasn't taking any chances.

I ran and ran, hoping the father's words meant they weren't chasing me. With several hundred yards between us, I fell down behind a tree, my chest heaving and my head throbbing. I put my fingers gingerly up to the side of my head where the rock had hit me. It was tender, but not bleeding. I noticed that I still had the bottle of Black Water in my other hand. My fear turned to relief at my escape and then to anger as I went back over what she had been doing out in the woods before I came up. What a hypocrite! Why had she judged me for swimming in the Black Water when she was drinking it? Why had she lied to her father and the other men and turned them against me? I opened the bottle and poured all of the Black Water on the ground.

Just then I heard a rustling in the trees, from the direction I had just come from. I ducked down, peering through the bushes. One of the men I had seen with the girl's father was moving slowly through the trees, a rock still in each of his hands. Why were they still hunting me? I could understand why the father would want to protect his daughter, but it seemed like he had delivered the message loud and clear. Why would this man pursue me with an obvious intention of hurting me? I might not be committed to the Hall anymore, but I certainly remembered that they did not condone violence in any way.

"Come out, you sinner," the man called out into the forest. He was still looking all around, so I didn't think he knew where I was. "We'll teach you to break away from the Hall of Good Works."

My mind raced. He was hunting me because he thought I was a threat to the Hall? That seemed ridiculous to me, but I remembered how often people in the Hall talked about the horrible things that people did in the Maze and sometimes it even included people outside the Hall. They would talk about people who compromised the true Path, and people who diluted the truth of Jesus. Is that what they thought I was doing? I was just trying to find the way Jesus wanted me to go. But if this man thought getting rid of me would somehow help purify the Hall, I didn't want to give him a chance to do that.

Crawling on my belly, I scooted back towards my right as quietly as I could. I thought that if I kept moving back towards my right, I would have to come across the Path of Trusting God. I only hoped the man wouldn't follow me there.

A few minutes later, I did come across the trail, and began to jog down the path more quickly now, leaving the man behind. As I jogged, all sorts of scenarios played through my mind. I still had the water bottle I had found, although it was empty now. What if I circled around and marched into the Hall of Good Works, pointed at the girl, and announced loudly that she was a Black

Water Drinker? He father wouldn't believe me, but I was sure others would. And I could have shown them the bruise where I had been hit with the rock, all for trying to expose her unrighteousness. If only the bottle was still full, so I could have poured that Black Water out on the pristine marble floors of the Hall? Or I could have thrown it in her face. No, that would have been a little too dramatic.

Of course, there was also the risk of running into more people like the man who was chasing me. It had never occurred to me that I might have enemies, or be in danger. I decided to give the Hall a wider berth from that day forward. I also realized that to accuse the girl was to go right back to playing the games of the Hall, and I would be the hypocrite this time.

I decided I was far enough away now and slowed to a walk. As I walked, my anger changed as it often did. I turned my anger on myself. Why had I been so blind? Why had I made myself so vulnerable? Why was I looking for some way to strike back at her when she is obviously hurting and desperate, just like I was not so long before?

I wasn't paying enough attention to where I was going until I recognized a fallen log next to the Path. It dawned on me with a start that I had come back down the Path of Good Works instead of up the Path of Trusting God, and there was the Pool of Black Water only a few dozen steps from where I stood. I had gotten my directions completely reversed. I should have turned around right then, but instead I made my way through the brush and sure enough, there it was.

I stood and I stared at it for the longest time. "I hate this water," I said to myself, reasoning things out in my head. "But it calls to me. Jesus has shown me how destructive it is. Do I care? I don't want to get into that water again. I remember the shame and guilt that I know will come. Is it worth it? Is this proof that the young man yesterday was right, that I'm not really fixed either? Is it proof that the girl was right –that I've just been deluding myself into thinking my new Path was better? If I swim now, won't I be doing exactly what she accused me of, using the grace I know Jesus will give me as an excuse to sin now?"

I thought about the water bottle full of this Black Water, and then I remembered the water bottle Jesus gave me. I opened it up and drank deeply. I could hear Jesus saying, "I love you. Do you believe me?" And, this time at least, the temptation to swim faded.

But, almost on a whim, I took the bottle the girl had left behind and refilled it with the Black Water, carrying it with me.

Chapter 6 – Frogs

The next morning I woke up slowly, my head still aching, but feeling good about myself otherwise. I had escaped the hunters from the Hall of Good Works, but even more spectacularly I had withstood the temptation to swim in the Black Water! It was hard to imagine that such willpower, such strength of character, could come from me! "Does this mean I really am fixed? Or at least something closer to it?" I wondered.

With a spring in my step, I set to work on my clay sculpture. I worked on Jesus' face, giving him a huge grin as he hugged me. He had made a good choice, saving me, I thought. Things were rough going there for awhile, but finally I was turning out to be something special after all.

I had a different perspective on the encounter with the girl and her father in my musings than I had the day before. I had been in the right, I decided, doing what I could to help her. They had shown their unrighteousness by attacking me. It was typical Hall-of-Good-Works-type behavior. I gingerly touched the bump on my head. "The marks of persecution," I thought to myself. That was just what happened when others saw the truth about people living on the Path of Trusting God and didn't understand or accept it. I decided that their attack was actually proof that I was in the right the whole time.

After lunch my head felt better, and I again decided to go exploring. This time I intentionally went in the direction of the Hall of Good Works. I had already forgotten my decision of the day before to stay away, and was caught up in my own delusions of grandeur. "Why, I bet I could walk right in there right now without a mask on and everyone would be amazed at the righteousness just radiating from my face! The girl and her father would even be forced to apologize to me for their mistake," I thought to myself.

I strode past the rock where I had met the girl, noting that there was no one there now. I surveyed the scene, picking up a few rocks that I thought might have been aimed at me if I hadn't run when I did. I tossed them up in the air, catching them on the way down, and dropped them into my knapsack. Sure, they added a little weight, but they also served to remind me of the day I had overcome both enemies and temptation.

I walked a little farther in the direction of the Hall, slower now. I heard voices up ahead. Soon I could see a group of people doing a very peculiar thing. It looked like they were painting trees. Some of the workers had brown paint and they were painting the trunks of the trees, while some of the workers had green paint and they were painstakingly painting the leaves, one at a time. This was especially remarkable when I noticed that some of them were painting the needles of the evergreen trees using tiny brushes.

As I approached, I could see that they were all wearing masks. "This is a work detail from the Hall of Good Works," I thought knowingly. They were "beautifying the forest" – making the grounds around the Hall pristine and perfect. I had been on a few such work details, though nothing as painstakingly detailed as this. Mostly, I had picked up trash, moved rocks that were misplaced, or raked leaves that had already fallen.

I walked right up to them and introduced myself, intentionally leaving out the fact that I had parted ways with the Hall. I figured that could be the dramatic twist after I had won them over with my charm and obvious show of righteousness. I shook hands all around. They were all doing fine. "Of course they are," I thought to myself, smiling knowingly. And of course I could truthfully say I was doing fine that day as well, meaning every word of it. If only they knew what it really meant to be fine the way I did.

"This is an amazing job you guys are doing painting these trees," I complimented. "It must take real skill and patience to paint each leaf individually with such detail."

"Thank you," one of the ladies responded politely. "It is arduous work, but it's worth it in order to serve the Lord."

That was my queue. "Of course, and I'm not doubting your sincerity, mind you, but it seems to me that the trees are already so beautiful without the painting. After all, the Lord made them that way in the first place. In fact, he's made all kinds of beautiful things, and some of them aren't even anywhere near the Hall. I've seen waterfalls, rock formations, and beautiful valleys full of wildflowers that were just spellbinding. I've seen a lot more of God's creation out there than I ever could have just staying on the grounds here like you are. In fact, I've found real happiness just walking with Jesus. Again, I'm not trying to put down what you're doing here. I'm just wondering if there is something better you could be doing with your time."

One of the men turned to me, setting his paintbrush carefully on the edge of his paint can and taking a step in my direction. "Look here, I think you need to understand something. We all know there are some beautiful things out there. But we also understand that just wandering around looking for such things is really a selfish thing to do. It's not helping anybody but yourself. What we do here is done to worship God and to help the others who live and stay in the Hall where they belong.

There may be beautiful things out there, but there are also dangerous and evil things out there. We sacrificially work to protect those weaker than us from those dangers by making sure all their needs are met right here on the grounds where it is safe."

"I can certainly appreciate that," I said, a little unsure of myself now. "But if by dangerous things you're talking about things like the Pools of Black Water, I've found the strength to resist that temptation. I'm sure I can withstand anything else that comes along."

"Black Water?" one of the other men said gruffly. "Hmmph. Never touch the stuff. Disgusting if you ask me. I don't know why anybody would ever even be tempted by that."

"Now be fair," said the lady who had graciously received my compliment before. "Of course *we* might see how disgusting that stuff is, but some people are weaker than us. That's exactly what we're talking about, what we want to protect them from."

"Well," I said defensively, taken aback. "We've all got something, you know. We're all weak, as you call it, in something. Maybe for me it's Black Water. But for you it's something else."

"I don't know what it could be," he responded. "I've lived on the straight and narrow my whole life." Several others gave agreeable nods.

I was startled by the strength of his resolve. "You mean you don't struggle with temptations of any kind?"

"Only if doing Works for the Lord is a temptation." Everyone else laughed.

"Don't you ever feel depressed, or bitter, or angry, or unloved, or anything like that?" I queried, feeling like I've been backed into a corner.

He laughed, "Nope. I'm as happy as a clam on Tuesday."

I was stunned. Here was a group of people who were apparently living successfully on the Path of Satisfying God. They didn't struggle the way I did. I couldn't understand how this could be so, because if some people could do it, then everybody should be able to do it. We shouldn't need the Path of Trusting God at all. We shouldn't need grace as a fallback. Surely these people were hiding something.

So I pushed forward, looking for a chink in their armor, "Then why are you still wearing the mask then? At least I've taken off the mask!"

The man shook his head, "I think you better think again before you start making accusations. I'm not the one wearing a mask. You are!"

I reacted instinctively by putting my hand to my face and was shocked to feel the smooth, hard edges of a mask on my own face! When did I put that on? I felt ridiculous talking to this group of righteous workers. I felt cornered. All I wanted to do was get away from that place and those people. Backing away, I ripped the mask from my face, threw it on the ground, and turned to run back into the trees. I could hear the group murmuring behind me and I could just imagine what they must be saying about me.

"What a failure!"

"Imagine lying to oneself like that!"

"People like that don't even deserve to have crossed the bridge!"

"No fruit in that life, that's for sure!"

"God must be so disappointed!"

"Now that one needs to straighten up and start living right. Imagine, going down into that disgusting Black Water!"

Of course, they were right. Just like the girl's father was right. And the girl herself was right about the Path of Trusting God. I felt so ridiculous, having strutted into that group like I had it all together. They should have started throwing stones too. I deserved it.

I made my way back to my camp without seeing anyone else. I was glad, because I didn't want to talk to anyone anymore. As I entered my camp, my eyes fell on the clay sculpture I had made; only now I looked at it with contempt. I was appalled at the ridiculous shaping of Jesus' face with the big smile on it. To fix it, I took two fingers and crudely reshape the smile into a deep frown. "Jesus is so disappointed by me," I thought. "Why did he even give me that hug? It must have just been pity."

Then I dropped down to the ground and began to sob. I was filled with repulsion for myself. I wept until I had nothing left. After my long walk and then an even longer cry, my throat was dry and sore. I remembered that I had two water bottles – one Jesus gave me, and the Black Water I had saved.

After a brief moment of indecision, I opened the bottle of Black Water and I drank deeply. It tasted slightly salty, leaving me still feeling thirsty even after drinking half the bottle.

I sat there and drank until the whole bottle was empty, just staring at the clay sculpture I had made. I was such a fool. Why did I ever think Jesus could actually love me? I thought about how I wasn't able to help the young man or the young woman. In fact, I had been very judgmental toward the young woman when I found out she still had sin in her life, even though I did too. I had puffed myself up with pride after her father accused me falsely, but it turned out that he was right. I had thought myself something pretty special when I had resisted the pool of Black Water, but I hadn't really resisted it at all. It all became clear when I met this group painting the trees - they were the real deal. They had found a way to fix themselves, if there had ever been anything to fix in the first place. I could never hope to live up to their standards.

And where did that mask I was wearing come from? When had I put that on? I could only think it came from my false bravado as I deluded myself into thinking I was special. Or maybe it even came from convincing myself that Jesus loved me! Maybe it came from making that stupid sculpture!

That sculpture! Suddenly, I hated it more than I had ever hated anything in my entire life! I stood up and deliberately chose a log off my wood pile. Walking over to the sculpture, I used the log with a sawing motion to cleave the sculpture in two, as close to the middle as I could manage. Then I dragged the part that was "me" off the rock pedestal and dropped it unceremoniously several feet away. I took the mangled Jesus with his hideous frown and I turned him around so that his back was to me.

Then, almost as an afterthought, I took the empty bottle of Black Water and I placed it right in the middle, between us.

"There," I said out loud. "Now that is art."

Without any warning that anyone was there, I heard a voice from behind me. "I liked it better the first time."

I spun around, and standing there was Jesus. Why did he always appear when I least wanted him to? How long had he been there? He had obviously seen what I did to the sculpture. Had he seen me drink the Black Water? For a moment shame washed over me, but then I pushed it down and embraced the anger that was rising up in me instead. I was in the middle of a great pity-party and here he was to put the kibosh on the whole thing. And I was just really getting going!

Jesus continued, seeming to ignore my obvious anger and bad mood. "I'm not much of an art critic, but this just isn't right at all. Why did you put this bottle of Black Water between us? Didn't I tell you that we were on the same side of your sin from now on?"

"Yes, you did," I grumbled. "But it doesn't feel like it. If we're on the same side, why didn't you show up and stop me before I drank it? Or before I put it into the bottle? Or before I made a fool of myself in front of those righteous know-it-alls outside the Hall of Good Works? Why do you only show up after I've made a total mess of things?"

Jesus wasn't shaken by my outburst, but instead pressed on, "I also told you that you would never be alone, didn't I? I was with you through all of those things. It doesn't matter how long I was standing here," he answered the question I had only thought in my head and never verbalized, "because I am with you always. You just weren't paying attention to me. Instead, you were seeing what you wanted to see."

"Yeah?" I brooded, challenging him. "And what did I want to see, exactly?"

Jesus continued despite my stubbornness, "You wanted to see yourself as a sinner who is trying to be good. And when you felt like you were being good, you thought that made you a good and righteous person. And when you felt like you were being bad, then you beat yourself up about it and punished yourself by doing things to prove how bad you were."

Jesus' words took a moment to digest. This was not at all what I thought he was going to say. But I wasn't ready to concede yet. Finally, I reply with some reasoning of my own. "Now, when I met you on the bridge, when I came out of the maze, I wasn't a very good person, was I?"

Jesus chuckled, "No, you weren't. You were totally self-absorbed and determined to find your own path."

"Yes," I continued. "And I ended up wandering from place to place letting my sin get me in more and more trouble, right?"

I'm sure Jesus knew exactly where I was going with my reasoning, but he just nodded, letting me plow ahead.

"So now what am I doing? I've been wandering around from place to place, letting my sin get me in more and more trouble! So how can I be anything different now than the sinner that I was before?"

If Jesus was surprised at the veracity of my outburst, he didn't show it. Calmly, he responded, "You're still looking at this whole thing like the goal in life is to become a good and righteous person. It's not."

That caught me off guard. Just when I thought I had a good argument, Jesus had to go and change the parameters! "I know you've said things like that before," I answered slowly, "but I just have a hard time seeing how it works in practical life. What else should my goal be, if not to make the right choices and be a good person?"

Jesus smiled. "You're goal is to get to know me better. You're goal is to believe that I love you, and practice loving me in return."

I slumped down to the ground, exhausted both physically by my tantrum and emotionally by the struggle I always seemed to have in understanding what Jesus wanted from me. "And that will somehow fix me?" I pleaded.

Jesus came over and sank down beside me. "Why are you so obsessed with being 'fixed', as you put it?"

"Don't you want me to get over all this stuff that's weighing me down, Jesus? Don't you want me to be whole and right and good?"

Jesus said, "Of course I look forward to seeing who you will become, who I already know you will become. But I'm not just interested in the final product. I'm interested in the process. I'm interested in each little hill and valley we go through together on the journey, not just getting to a final destination."

I shook my head. "That sounds good, but I just don't get it. I would think you would be disappointed in me when I fail, so you would want to transform me into someone who doesn't fail as quickly as possible."

"That's Hall of Good Works thinking. It's pragmatism, defining the process as simply the shortest path to where you want to get. But each step in the process is just as important, just as exciting, in itself, without worrying about where it will take you in the end.

"Think about it this way. When you try to be a good person, you're natural inclination is to hide it when you do something bad, right?"

I nodded, so he continued, "You want to always have your best face on, so you only want others to see the part of you that is beautiful and not the part that is ugly. You are reasoning that if you can keep that up long enough, the beautiful will overcome the ugly and you will become the person you've been pretending to be all along. The problem with that theory is that when you hide your sin, you actually give strength to it. You give it power over you. You are like a scrawny little kid getting in the ring with a sumo wrestler. You may try your best to fight it, but you are going to lose."

I nodded in agreement again. "That's exactly what's been happening. Do you how many times I've let that Black Water beat me?"

Jesus chuckled, "No, I don't. I mean, I could give you a factual answer, but the truth is that I'm not keeping count. And I'm not holding it against you."

"So what do I do now?" I asked.

"You need to bring your sin out into the open. When you stop hiding it, it actually loses power over you. You shrink the sumo before you get in the ring with him."

I countered, "But I did bring it out into the open. I told those tree-painters all about it. And they threw it back in my face. And I told the young woman about it, and she used it against me."

Jesus looked amused. "I seem to recall that what you told the tree painters was that you had beaten it. That's not really the same thing as confessing it. Even then, I'm not sure those guys were the best ones to be sharing your deepest secrets with. They don't know what to do with it. The same goes for the young woman. It may have been helpful for her to hear your confession in the right circumstances, but at the time you were looking for some sort of approval from her. You were trying to use it to score points and win an argument. That never works."

I began to grow frustrated again, "Then how am I supposed to know who to tell and who not to tell?"

Jesus responded, "You tell people within the parameters of a trusting relationship. You tell people who care about you and who want to help you on your journey. But most of all, you tell me. Remember, I am with you always. You can talk to me anytime, even if you don't see me. And someday, when you are relying on me for your approval and not looking to other people, then you might tell someone like the young woman in order to invite her in to trust me with her own struggles, but not to prove a point."

My mind went back to the tree-painters. "The group I met from the Hall of Good Works is made up of good people. They've done the whole good works/satisfying God thing and it's worked for them. It was so humiliating to compare myself to them."

Jesus put his arm around my shoulders. "So stop comparing yourself to them, then. It seems like you're complaining because they are really good at playing a game that I'm not paying any attention to. Look, when I say that I care more about an honest relationship with you than I do about how good of a person you are, that's not just a saying to placate you when you are down. The same is true for everybody, even those who are succeeding at being good people, as you call them. How well someone plays that game doesn't negate the fact that the game itself is broken."

"It's like that little square of sky that you found and gazed at when you were still in the maze," Jesus suggested. "You knew that little square was part of a much bigger whole that you couldn't see, and you had to be satisfied with just that small part. Experiencing that small amount of sky was certainly something when that's all you had, but it wasn't enough to satisfy you. The life I have for you is like the whole, great sky stretching out before you. You could choose a little square and stay in that and say that you were indeed living within my plan, but you would be missing out on so much more by not stretching out and taking in the whole sky."

My puzzlement must have shown on my face, because Jesus switched tactics.

"I want to show you something," he announced as he stood up, pulling him up with him. We walked over to the pool, looking down into the clear, cool water. "What do you see here?" Jesus asked.

"I see tadpoles," I replied. "Lots of tadpoles swimming around. I've enjoyed watching them ever since I came here."

Jesus squatted down and dipped one finger into the water, watching the tadpoles swim away in all directions. After a few seconds, they forgot about the finger intruding into their home and went back to their seemingly mindless wandering. A couple of them swam around Jesus' finger, exploring it momentarily before swimming away.

"These tadpoles have a lot of limitations, don't they?" Jesus mused. "They can't walk or run or fly, or even hop. They are trapped in this tiny pool, totally dependent on it for their survival. They can't look elsewhere for food. They can't even imagine what is outside of this pool. It's the only world they know. But do you know what you would find if you could look at their DNA?"

"What?" I asked, interested, as I squatted down next to him.

"Frogs. If you looked at the DNA of these tadpoles and the DNA of a fully formed frog, they would be identical. If you had the ability to look at the DNA and use that blueprint to re-create it into a living creature, you would come up with a frog. You would never in a million years think there was a tadpole in there."

"That's amazing," I say. "But what does it have to do with me?"

"When you look at you, you see a tadpole. You only know the world by the small perspective you know, but you act as if it is really everything there is. And you look at those guys up there in the Hall of Good Works as being some of the best tadpoles ever, because they are really good at living within the limited parameters you have accepted as reality. But I know there is so much more to life, so much in fact that tadpoles swimming in a little pool seem like a sad, little sight. But when I look at you, I see a frog. I see you transformed into what you are designed to be. What is even the best tadpole in the world if it never transforms into a frog? And what good is it to become a frog if you stay in the pool with the tadpoles and never leave?

"The things you told that young man up on the mountain were true. His struggle is that he can't believe it's this simple, and neither can you. He's trying to turn it into a formula so that he can still control it. There's no controlling it. You just need to trust me to love you through this journey. That encounter showed that you know everything you need to know. You just have to keep putting it into practice and forgive yourself when you mess up."

"OK, "I said slowly. "So then here's me trusting you. Here's me being honest. I'm weak and I really love the way Black Water makes me feel. When I'm depressed or lonely or frustrated or whatever, I know it will make me feel better for awhile. Some days I might be able to resist it, like I did yesterday. But I'm just as likely to give in to the temptation. I am jealous of people who don't struggle, and I am judgmental of people who do struggle. There. That's me being honest. And it feels pretty ugly. So now what?"

"Now," Jesus answered, "you accept yourself for who you really are. You're not a tadpole, you're a frog. You're not a 'not-very-good-person trying to be very good'. You're not even a sinner in need of help to be a saint. Instead, you are a saint who still fails. A frog still sticking close to the pool because it is all it's ever known. Do you see the difference? Accept that you are a person loved by God and made righteous by God. Accept that you are a new creation. Accept that your identity is found in relationship with me. That will take your focus off your fight with sin. And you will learn to find better answers to the emotional needs that you have. You will not be as preoccupied with pleasing others or as afraid of their criticism. You will find that the desire for sin fades as you let me fulfill your desires instead."

I swallowed. "OK. But what if it's not enough? What if I mess up again?"

Jesus laughed at that, lightening the mood. "Oh, you will. I want you to accept that messing up doesn't change who you are in me. It doesn't change my love for you, or my joy in spending time with you." Standing up, he announced, "Now let me help you fix the mess you made of this sculpture!"

Chapter 7 – Paul

Life settled down a lot after that. I intentionally focused on implementing the things Jesus had told me. Not a day went by that I didn't spend time watching the tadpoles, excitedly watching as some began to grow legs and visibly transform into the frogs they were meant to be. I stayed away from the forest near the Hall of Good Works, not sure if I was ready for another encounter. I also stayed away from the Pool of Black Water, fully aware that I could not trust myself. If I gave in to temptation, it would hurt me and my relationship with Jesus. If I resisted by my own willpower, the results could be just as harmful as my pride puffed up in me.

I also generally avoided other people, wary of just about anyone I met. I got to know the names of a few people who lived nearby, but never became more than passing acquaintances. Each day, I made many short hikes up and around my campsite next to the pool and waterfall, but always returned to the same place each evening. My sculpture was completed with the help of Jesus, and his smiling face as he embraced me was the centerpiece for the whole camp.

And that was life for many months. It was uneventful and in many ways fulfilling to me as I grew in my relationship with Jesus. But at the same time, I still felt like something was missing. I couldn't put my finger on it, but now I know that I was lonely. And it was more than just loneliness. I longed to have someone else who was truly on the same path as I was who could identify with and help me in my walk with Jesus. Someone like the strange young man trying to control his walk with Jesus couldn't understand what I was going through. Neither could someone like the girl hiding her secret sin but still living in the Hall of Good Works. And I certainly couldn't benefit from spending time with those who were successful in living on the Path of Satisfying God. All of those people might be people I could help if and when I was stronger in my own journey, but I longed for someone who could be of help to me first. That's when I met Paul.

It was a hot, sticky afternoon when I set out that day. Emotionally, I was not doing well. It wasn't that anything in particular had happened; just that it was a really bad day. I was feeling very lonely and a lot of my old insecurities were clamoring for attention. I could hear the voices clearly. "You're not good enough. You'll never be good enough. Nobody loves you. Jesus is so disappointed in you. Those Tree-Painters are so much better than you are. You're worthless. Why do you even try?" And so forth. I tried to block them out but it was like they were screaming in my head. I prayed to Jesus to help me, but he was silent. Only I guess he was listening after all.

So I started walking. It was one of those strange times when I knew exactly where I was going – I was going to the Pool of Black Water – but I was pretending that I didn't know. I told myself that I was just out for a walk. I wouldn't let my conscious mind even think the words "Black Water", but I can admit now that there was no doubt where I was going to end up. It was exactly what Jesus had told me – that when I felt like I was a bad person, I would do things to prove to myself how bad I was. And in the moment, I didn't care. I was beyond responding to what Jesus had already told me.

As I walked though, I was brought out of my stupor by the sound of somebody crying out, "Help! Help!" I looked around, and as far I as could tell, I was alone. Then I hear it again,

"Help!" The sound was coming from over to my left, off the trail.

"Where are you?" I called out.

"Down here! I'm at the bottom of the hill!"

And sure enough, there was a steep embankment at the edge of the path and a man lying at the bottom. I clambered down to him. He said that he had stepped on a loose rock on the trail, lost his footing, and rolled down the hill. He banged his leg on a rock, and thought it might be broken.

"You sure are lucky I came along," I exclaimed. How long were you down here?"

"Only about five minutes," he said. "But I don't think luck had anything to do with it. If God hadn't brought you here, there might not have been anybody else for days."

I didn't tell him why I was on that trail in the first place. I liked the idea that God was using me to help this man a lot better than thinking I was rebelling against God and falling back into my sinful habits.

I helped him back up the hill and back to my camp. His leg wasn't broken, and he was back to walking around in a few days. His name was Paul. He was sixty-two years old. And he had lived the first fifty-five years of his life in the Hall of Good Works.

It was amazing to me how open Paul was about himself. He had a certain confidence that you could tell came from his relationship with Jesus. He talked as casually about his own failings as he would about the weather. But he wasn't complaining or making excuses or anything like that. He was just so enthralled with what Jesus had done in his life that everything else seemed inconsequential.

"It hasn't always been so," he said as we sat around the campfire the very first night I found him. "Until recently, I was completely immersed in the Good Works Lifestyle. I grew up in it. I kept every rule ever made. Every jot and tittle, as they say. I became one of the youngest managers the Hall has ever known. I won several awards for my service over the years. I was admired by everyone. I reached a point where young men competed to be under my supervision, and I only chose the best and brightest to work under me."

"But," Paul said, "I was miserable. I just didn't know it. I didn't really know God, and I was too caught up in myself to even realize that. I thought I was the bee's knees, which is exactly what everybody else kept telling me too, and that was the problem."

"What happened to change all that?" I asked, passing him a mug of hot cocoa.

"Well, the short answer is Jesus. Jesus happened. But that's not what it seemed like at the time. At the time I would have said it was devil, and I thought I was losing everything. You see, about seven years ago, my perfect life came completely unraveled.

"I was training a group of young men to be prayer leaders. We met every day. It was a lot more intensive than simply teaching them prayer techniques or leadership skills. I was teaching them how to live the Good Works Lifestyle. I was very involved in their lives, dictating almost every minute of their days and keeping them accountable to me for all of their behavior. I had done the same thing with more boys than I can count. I had developed an iron-clad system and could proudly point to many of the Hall's leaders as being graduates of my program.

"But this particular group was different. Rather, I should say that one young man in this group was different. The rest of the group worked hard to toe the line just as I expected them to. But this young man was a special case. He was known to be unruly and difficult even before he entered my program. Normally, I wouldn't have wasted my time on him, but his father had been an old friend of mine. He had died when the boy was young, which is what I attributed his rebellion to. I thought I could make a difference and turn the boy around when everyone else had given up on him. I see now that it was still my pride and not real concern for the boy that motivated my decision to mentor him.

"We had problems from day one. He was often late, skipped work assignments, and talked back when I reprimanded him. He did not like to be told what to do, and I was used to being obeyed without question. I became more and more frustrated with him, but my reaction was to just push harder and make the punishments for his misbehavior harsher. I can admit now that I began to enjoy watching him suffer for his insubordination, and became more and more creative in my punishments."

Paul paused in his story as I dished up the soup that had been simmering over the fire, and we both ate in silence. I've always been amazed at how good even simple foods taste when they are cooked outside over an open fire. But it tasted even better to be able to share it with someone else, someone like Paul.

Paul sopped up the last of his soup with a piece of bread and shoved it in his mouth. He had barely swallowed when he resumed his story. He picked it up like he had never stopped at all. "So it all came to a head one day when the young man did not show up for the accountability group until he was more than two hours late. I did not even give him a chance to explain. Instead, I assumed his behavior was more of the same shenanigans he was always pulling, and berated him harshly in front of all the other students. I was shocked this time when the boy reacted differently than normal. Instead of staring me down defiantly, he only looked at the floor where large teardrops were falling from his eyes. If I had not been caught up in my own hubris, I might have been clued in that something else was going on. Instead, I relished the idea that the tears were a sign I had finally broken his rebellious spirit. I finished my tirade and sent him off to work duty.

"I went back to my office during my lunch break to find a note from the boy's family manager. The young man's mother had passed away unexpectedly the night before. The note was excusing him from duty. I had no idea why he had even shown up at all, but I felt terrible for the way I had treated him.

"I went to find him immediately, pulling him off the work detail he was slaving through.

"'I just found out about your mom,' I said. 'Why didn't you tell me?'

"'I didn't get the chance,' he spat, returning to his usual irate self. 'You were too busy attacking me to listen.'

"'But why did you even come at all? You had an excuse from your family manager.'

"'I came because I thought you cared about me. I thought I could come to you. But you don't care at all, do you? All you care about is your precious reputation.'

"The damage was done. He harbored bitterness towards me from that day on, and I was too proud to apologize. A few weeks later, I was called to a board meeting. The boy had accused me of...well, let's just say of making inappropriate advances towards him. It was a complete fabrication, but there was not stopping it once it was out. The rumors spread. Soon everyone was suspicious. Other stories came up out of nowhere with nothing to substantiate any of them. I was stunned and hurt as people I thought were my friends turned their backs on me and added their own lies to the mix. It seemed like the more I protested, the more they believed I was guilty.

"When I just couldn't take it anymore, I ran. I left the Hall in the middle of the night without any idea where I would go. Best thing that ever happened to me," Paul said with a chuckle.

"Why? What happened?" I asked.

"I found Jesus. Or rather, he found me. When I left the Hall, I ran up into the hills, not sure where to go. I had never left the grounds before. I had no idea what was even out here. I had heard stories, rumors mostly, of demons and dangers lurking everywhere. I didn't think they could possibly all be true, but I honestly didn't know what to expect. That first night, I actually climbed up in a tree and tried to sleep, thinking it was safer than being on the ground!"

Seeing the grin on Paul's face, I chuckled along with him, thinking of the older man trying to lie between the branches of a tree.

"The next morning," Paul continued, "I was so stiff I could hardly walk. I had barely slept at all. I had brought enough food for about a day, and the same amount of water, but after that I knew I would have to find something. But I had no idea where to go. I was afraid of anyone I might meet, because I thought everybody out here would be monsters. On top of all that, I was emotionally a mess. I had lost everything that had been important to me. I felt like God had abandoned me even though I had been his star servant. I was angry and disillusioned and depressed. I was actually very close to suicide."

The matter-of-fact way Paul admitted the depths of his struggle made me uncomfortable. Most people would never confess such a thing, or, if they did, would either whisper it as some sort of dirty little secret or brag about it is a sort of twisted claim to fame. Paul did neither of these, but openly shared his suicidal thoughts as if they were just another part of the story.

"I wandered aimlessly farther and farther away from the Hall. The next night I chose to sleep on the ground, too exhausted to care what dangers were out there. I consumed the last of my food and water, telling myself this was my last meal. I didn't know how I would do it, but I fully intended to kill myself the next day. As I lay there with only a single blanket between me and the rest of the world, my anger broke. I started to cry, 'God, help me. God, if I've ever meant anything to you, help me now. I don't want to die. Please, show me the way.' I finally fell asleep still crying out that prayer.

"The next morning I woke up to the sound and smell of bacon frying! I sat up with a start to find a man sitting next to a campfire, with a skillet of bacon and eggs frying on a rock on one side. 'Who are you?' I asked.

"The man smiled at me and said, 'Oh good, you're awake. Breakfast is almost ready.' He pointed over one shoulder and added, 'There's a stream about fifty yards that way. Why don't you go freshen up while I finish these eggs? You smell…rather rank.' He smiled apologetically at this last part, but I knew he was right. I hadn't showered in a couple of days. What I didn't know was who he was.

"As I made my way down to the stream, I pondered who he could be. He didn't seem like a threat. In fact, he seemed like a friend, although I was sure I had never met him. Once I was out of his line of vision, I wondered if I should just leave. But I was really hungry, and his breakfast looked really good. What could it hurt to stay a few minutes? I found the stream just as he had said I would, and stripped off my shirt before dunking my head completely into the clear water. It was refreshing. I finished cleaning up but had to put the same clothes back on. Then I made my way back to the campfire. The man already had a plate served up for me, and I sat down on the ground and took it from him.

"It was the best food I've ever tasted. That might be because I was so hungry, but I'm not sure. I gobbled it down as fast as I could. When I was done, I said, 'Thank you. But I still don't know who you are."

"'I think you know,' he said kindly. 'You just don't know that you know. I've come to answer your prayer from last night.'

"'What? My prayer? You mean...you're an angel are something? Sent from God?' I was incredulous, but at the same time secretly hopeful. Maybe God had heard my prayer after all. Maybe he did care about me.

"'Better,' he laughed.

"'Then you're...Jesus?" I asked.

"'The One and Only!' he responded enthusiastically.

"Now I was sure this was a joke. I had never heard of someone meeting Jesus face to face. I thought this must be the kind of cruel prank people out here in this wasteland must play on people like me. I expected a group of laughing hooligans to jump out at any second and beat me senseless with clubs. 'Who are you really?' was all I could say.

"What happened next is very hard to describe. The man's appearance began to change. It was as if a light began to shine out from him, without any obvious source. The only thing I could think about was how glorious he looked. Holy. All my life I had thought that I was righteous because of the life I had lived, but this was the real deal. My efforts to duplicate it with mere actions were ridiculous when compared to who I was beholding. In just a matter of seconds, I became fully convinced that this was indeed Jesus. And I was not worthy to be in his presence.

"Suffice it to say that Jesus showed me how my whole way of life had been a lie from the beginning. I had become very good at wearing a very particular mask – a mask that everybody loved. I had basked in the adoration and respect that people had for that mask. I even believed the mask was the real me. But when those accusations came, the mask was ruined. I didn't know the real me, and neither did anybody else. Nobody would stand up for me because it was the mask they loved, not me. When the mask was tarnished, they were quick to distance themselves and throw stones in order to keep their own masks in place.

"Jesus taught me a different way of living, and a different way of looking at myself. If I see myself through his eyes, I am a child of God, heir to all his promises. Compared to that, none of the good works I was doing were worth much anyway. I really didn't fall as far as I thought I had, and it turned out to be the beginning of a whole new way of living."

So that was Paul. He became my best friend. And although he doesn't like titles, he also became my mentor. But it's not what I would have expected, because he never chastised me when I messed up or gave me tips on how to do better. He didn't come to me with a list of demands or things I needed to fix. Instead, he accepted and loved me for who I was almost as much as Jesus did.

I remembered the friend I had back when I still lived in the maze – Mark. But I had to say that both of us were a lot more committed to living our lifestyle than we were to each other. As long as the two were compatible, we were fine. But if they weren't, all bets were off. If there was only enough room for one in the pool, we fought like cats and dogs. I was fully aware that Mark would betray me in order to help himself without a second thought, and I would do the same to him. But the good thing about Mark was that he would never judge me. He didn't care that I smelled like Black Water or anything else because so did he. He didn't care what I did. In fact, if we did fight over something, we were back to being pals as soon as whatever we were fighting about was gone.

I hadn't found anything like that on the mountain trails, except for Jesus. That was why it was so hard to finally tell Paul the truth about myself. I didn't want him to be disappointed in me. I didn't want him to leave me alone again. But he was always saying how much he appreciated me and how I had helped him that day when he fell. He was always saying how God had sent me down that path that day, just to help him. Finally, I couldn't take it anymore.

"Paul," I said one day. "I need to tell you something. God didn't send me down that path to help you. I wasn't listening to God very well that day. In fact, I was on my way down to the Pool of Black Water."

"Why were you going there?" he asked.

"Well, to swim in it," I admitted. "When I was in the maze, that's all my life was. I went from one Black Water Pool to the next. I know now that I'm different – that Jesus made me different – but I don't always feel like it. And sometimes I still fail."

"I see," he said. "OK, but I still say God brought you to help me."

"What?" I exclaimed. "Weren't you listening? I was in a bad place. If anything, God pushed you down that hill so you would rescue me!"

Paul laughed. "Maybe so. Maybe we were there for each other."

But I wasn't satisfied. "Aren't you going to tell me how bad that is? Aren't you going to tell me how I can't do that anymore? Aren't you going to tell me you can't stay with me if I can't control myself?"

And Paul laughed again. "Why would I say any of that? I'm really glad you trusted me with your struggle, because now maybe I can help you when you are in trouble. But chastising you or distancing myself from you isn't going to help either of us. That's the same thing the people in the Hall did to me."

"No it isn't," I argued. "You were innocent. I'm not."

"I wasn't innocent. I may not have done the particular things they were accusing me of, but I was far from innocent. The fact of the matter is that I was in trouble and could have used a friend, but I didn't have one. But now I do have one, and so do you."

Since that day I've never doubted Paul's love for me again. Sure, we don't always agree. But we always have each other's backs. And it has sort of become a fun little argument we have over and over. He will say how God sent me down that path to rescue him from his fall, and I'll say that God pushed him down that hill to rescue me.

Times were good with just the two of us. But God had plans to add a third to the mix.

Chapter 8 – Mary

Paul and I were hiking through the woods when we came upon
her. Rather, I should say that she caught us. Without warning,
tin cans in the trees above us started shaking, making a loud
rattling sound. I looked over at Paul and he pointed at his feet.
He had tripped over a hidden piece of string, setting off the
warning bells.

Before we could register what had happened, a girl appeared in
front of us brandishing a sharpened stick. Her face was
scratched and filthy and her clothes were torn and covered in
dirt and grime. She tried to appear tough, but it was obvious
that she was terrified of us. It struck me that there was
something oddly familiar about her, but I couldn't quite put my
finger on it.

"Get back!" she cried, waving the stick around. I was all for
turning around and leaving this girl behind before somebody
got hurt, but Paul put a hand on me.

"We don't want to hurt you," he said. "We're here to help, if
you want it."

"I don't need any help from you," she spat. And suddenly I
recognized her. She was the crying girl I had met by the rock –
the one who was so judgmental about the Path of Trusting God.
She was the one who had lied about me to her father, and
almost gotten me stoned! She was the one who was secretly
drinking Black Water! I had certainly never expected to see her
again, especially not under these circumstances. I didn't know

what she was doing living out here, but I wasn't interested in finding out either.

"Let's go," I said to Paul. "She's trouble."

But Paul was paying attention only to the girl. Shrugging me off, he said, "I think you do need some help. You're obviously very afraid. We can help you with whatever it is you're afraid of."

She waved the stick around some more. "I just want you to leave," she snarled.

"You heard her," I said. "She just wants us to leave. "

But then the girl recognized me, too! "Hey, I know you," she said, turning to wave the stick in my direction. "You're that goody-two-shoes who bragged about swimming in the Black Water!"

I was getting angry, "Yeah, and you're the lying hypocrite who drinks it!"

She flinched. I had hit a nerve. I expected her to become even more riled up, but instead she recoiled, and started crying again.

"It's OK," Paul said. "I can tell something bad has happened to you, but we're not going to hurt you. I don't care what you have or haven't done. Let us help you." Paul pulled out his water bottle and held it out to the girl. She hesitated, then, still crying, she lowered the stick and took the water bottle. It seemed Paul had broken through to her with his kindness, somehow.

I moved off and found a rock to sit on. Paul gave the girl some food and they talked together for a very long time. I sat there brooding, playing back the events of our first encounter in my head over and over. What was she doing out here now? I knew she must be playing at something, I just wasn't sure what. All I knew was that she couldn't be trusted, and she must have an ulterior motive. I watched the two of them, and eventually Paul leaned over with a smile and gave the girl a big hug. "You don't know what you're doing," I said under my breath. "Just wait and she'll stab you in the back."

Then Paul stood up and walked over to me. He sat down beside me. "You wanna tell me about it?" he asked.

I told him of how I had met the girl, thinking she was on our side when really she was from the Hall of Good Works. I told him all of the horrible things she had said about people on this Path. I told him how I had tried to be honest with her about my struggles, and how she had turned it against me. She had made me look like a fool. She had told lies about me and almost gotten me killed. And then, I had found the bottle of Black Water she had been secretly drinking; only she said it was mine!

"That sounds like a frustrating experience," Paul said when I had finished. "But it also sounds like you've held onto it for way too long. Are you ready to forgive her yet?"

"Why?" I asked. "What's her story now?"

"It doesn't matter," Paul said simply. "Even if we hadn't found her today, you would need to forgive her, for your sake. Forgiveness is a lot more powerful than most people think it is. Most of the time, we think holding a grudge gives us power, but it's really the other way around. Keeping that bitterness and frustration pent up inside you is eating you up, making you weaker and making it harder for you to focus on Jesus, because your focus is divided. Does that make sense?"

"I guess so," I mumbled, not ready to commit just yet. I hadn't been aware that I was holding a grudge. Most days I didn't give the girl a second thought. It was only seeing her that had brought it back.

Paul continued, "The fact of the matter is this – you have needed to forgive her for your own sake for a long time, and it has never been contingent on whether or not she asks for it. If someone has to ask your forgiveness before you will give it, then you're missing something important in your walk with Jesus. Jesus has never waited for people to come looking for forgiveness. The good news he shares with people is that God is not holding people's sins against them, remember? It doesn't matter if she has a had a change of heart, or if she is still living in the Hall of Good Works and coming out here to spy on us, or whatever else you might imagine. Regardless of her, you need to forgive her in order to move on with your own life. It's not saying that what she did was OK, but that you aren't going to hang on to your perceived right to judge and punish her. You need to give this pain and resentment you feel to God and trust him to heal you. If you hang onto it, the consequences will be worse than the original violation.

"Tell me, what did you do after your encounter with her?"

I tell him, "I went down to the Pool of Black Water, but I didn't get in. I resisted."

Paul smiled, "OK, but that tells you what kind of affect she had on you. She may be responsible for the words she said to you, but she's not responsible for how you react. And by how you behaved seeing her today, I'd say you're still reacting, maybe all along in ways you aren't consciously aware of. She's not responsible for that either. The only way you are going to be free of it is to own it and forgive her. Choose to release your hold on her as her judge and instead give that role to Jesus. And you know what Jesus has done with that role."

What Paul said made sense. I hadn't actually realized that I still harbored resentment toward her, but as I thought about it, I was really using her to personify my resentment at everyone in the Hall of Good Works. It certainly wasn't fair to her, and I hadn't realized I was holding a grudge against the Hall until now.

I won't say that it was easy, but as Paul and I sat there, I began to pray. Talking to Jesus, I forgave the girl for ridiculing me, and I forgave the men for how they had treated me, and I even forgave the Hall for how they taught people to judge the path that I was on, and for how they had treated Paul. It helped to realize that nobody there was malicious towards me directly, and that they were just doing what they thought was right to help people. I could see why the men thought I was some sort of predator or threat, and that they had been trying to protect the girl. But that led me to realize I needed to repent for my judgmental attitudes towards them. I might have hope that I could be reconciled with the young lady, but I realized that my forgiveness of the Hall was completely one-sided. Even if I could try to talk to someone there, it would be beyond their comprehension to accept what I was saying.

I shouldn't give the impression that all that happened while I sat there on that rock with Paul, either. It took a long time, and even now I have moments when I have to remind myself and forgive them all over again. But the beginnings of forgiveness started there as Paul helped me to see how I had held onto that grudge for so long.

And only after Paul was convinced that I was on the right track did he bring me to talk with the young lady. I see now why he wanted me to forgive first, because that way it was a more meaningful and sacrificial choice on my part. As I got to know her and hear her story, it was easy to have compassion for her, but she was a long ways from realizing I even wanted an apology.

Her name was Mary. At first all she really wanted to say was that she had left the Hall to live on her own. She was obviously scared of anybody and anything here outside of the Hall, so it didn't make any sense that she had left. But Paul said not to push her. So we helped her instead. We showed her where to get food and how to set up camp. She didn't know anything about living out here, and things had been a lot harder for her than they would have for someone more experienced. We showed her various trails to follow. We talked to her about Jesus' love and grace, and how he was transforming us. She was always very interested in Paul's stories from the Hall, and remembered when he had been ostracized. She had still been a kid, and had always assumed the Hall's side of the story. Hearing what Paul had to say went a long ways towards helping her see that they weren't as infallible as she thought. But she was very quiet about her own story.

It wasn't until a couple of months had gone by that she finally opened up. One morning, as I was cleaning up from breakfast, she approached me saying, "It was my water bottle you found that day we met."

"I know that," I answered. "I knew that right away. And it made me angry that you lied. You caused me a lot of trouble." I was surprised at how calmly I was able to say it, sharing the truth of my feelings without being accusatory. "I understand the pain and fear you must been feeling at the time. I get that you were trying to protect yourself."

Mary nodded, then took a breath and continued. I got the impression she had been rehearsing this speech for a while now. "I had been drinking the water secretly for a long time. I really did totally believe everything the Hall told me about how to live, but I just couldn't keep up. I had private feelings of worry, anxiety and fear that I couldn't talk about to anyone, because they made me seem weak. So instead I used the Black Water to medicate those feelings."

"I completely understand that, too," I told her. "I did the same thing, but then Jesus showed me that it wasn't really helping anything, and that I was better off trusting him with my pain," I said, and then added, "That sounds a lot simpler and a lot easier than it has been."

Soon after that, around the evening campfire, Mary sat down with Paul and me and finally told us what had happened to her. "My mother found my stash of Black Water in my room. She told my father, and they went to the managers. They were scared because of what it might mean for them and the rest of the family, but relieved when the manager assured them that I was the one to blame, not them. I was of age, and responsible for my own choices. I guess that much was true. But of course,

I couldn't stay. I wasn't even allowed to defend myself. My family, with the help of our family manager, sent me away."

I couldn't believe how much pain must be in this young lady's heart. One of the hardest things to see was that in a lot of ways she still thought they had been right. It was her fault. In her eyes, the Hall was righteous, so she didn't belong there. To her, being sent away was just like being thrown into the Black Abyss, and she was convinced that she deserved it. Even though she was desperate for Paul's and my help, she still thought of us as apostates of the faith.

I wouldn't have known how to help her if it hadn't been for Paul. On many occasions, he just told me to pray for her. There was one day when I left camp that I came across Jesus standing about a hundred yards away. I asked him what he was doing and he said that he wanted to help Mary, but that this was a close as she would let him get. She didn't understand how the real Jesus could be different from the Jesus taught about in the Hall, and she expected him to punish her just as severely.

On other days Paul led us to tell stories about our own adventures with Jesus, sharing with her but not pushing. She became more and more involved in the camp, doing her share of the chores and venturing out into the wild with less trepidation.

One night Mary asked Paul to tell her again of familiar story from when he had been in the Hall, the story of how he had first entered managerial training. It was a great story, I had to admit; even if it did idolize the pettiness often found in the Hall.

After a pause, Paul started in. "I was a young man, not much older than you, Mary. I was working hard in all my classes, and my teachers noticed my efforts. The time was quickly approaching when we would either be selected for our life tasks or be selected for further study. I wanted desperately to be chosen to continue my studies. Not only that, but I knew who I wanted my mentor to be. The great Mordecai!"

According to both Paul and Mary, Mordecai was a legendary leader in the Hall. He had passed away many years ago, but his portrait still hung in the library and his books were mandatory reading for many students. He was a tall, slender man with an air of dignity and class about him that made everyone else in the room feel as if they were in the presence of royalty, no matter who they were.

"But," continued Paul, "catching the attention of Mordecai was no easy matter. There were dozens of students vying for his tutelage, and he only chose a very select few. I knew I had the grades, but I needed something more if I wanted the coveted spot. So I figured, if I wanted Mordecai to like me, I needed to become more like Mordecai."

Mary laughed, knowing what was coming. "So what did you do?"

"Well, I already had the height, if not the slender build. So I started dieting furiously in an attempt to match his build. I cut and dyed my hair to match his salt-and-pepper tuft, and even grew a moustache to go along with it. So here I was, little more than a boy, groomed to look like a middle-aged man! Then I started practicing his walk, sort of a long but easy-going stride that fit his frame and personality. Learning to talk like him was a much harder challenge. He had a peculiar way of going up in pitch at the ends of certain words, and he never pronounced his 'r's. It took several weeks of practice, but I finally got to where I was doing a pretty good job, if I do say so myself. I even looked into some of his favorite hobbies, like sports, and took them up as well.

"My plan was to approach him at an upcoming function and introduce myself, all the while mimicking his looks and disposition. But as the date approached, I grew more and more nervous. I began to worry that he would think I was making fun of him with my imitation. I reasoned that my impersonation would have to be perfect, without a hint of exaggeration, in order to have the desired effect. I thought I was pretty good, but it didn't help that all my friends laughed whenever they saw me doing it. I needed some sort of objective test to know if I had it right.

"One of my friends had a solution. 'Paul,' he said one night over pizza, 'You would know that you had it right if you could fool someone who knows Mordecai, but doesn't know you or what you're doing. Why don't you try your impression on some of his personal attendants?'"

"It sounded like a brilliant idea to me. I chose an hour of the day when I knew Mordecai would be teaching, then I approached his personal suite in my best efforts at impersonation.

"The door was open, so I entered with the confidence of someone who walks through that door every day. I was met by a group of workers busily cleaning his rooms. At first they all stopped what they were doing and looked up at me intently. I thought the ploy was up just that fast. But then one man took a step towards me and said, 'Sir, we apologize for the intrusion. We did not expect you to be home so early.'"

"'Quite all right,' I said in my best imitation of Mordecai's voice. 'I have simply returned home for a moment in order to retrieve a particular item that escaped my attention this morning when I was gathering my things. Carry on.'"

"They seemed satisfied, because they all turned back to their various chores. I was elated. I strode purposefully over to a door on my left, hoping it was the bedroom or study and not a closet! As luck would have it, I was alone in Mordecai's bedroom. I decided that I should wait a couple of minutes, and then planned to walk back out as though I had retrieved whatever it was that I had forgotten. As I stood there, though, my stomach began to rumble. The pizza was not settling well on my nervous stomach. I realized with a shock that I needed the restroom immediately!"

With these words and Paul's improvisation as he grasped at his stomach, Mary and I both began to laugh. We knew this story, and knew the best was still to come.

"I found the bathroom right off of the bedroom, and went in to take care of business. When I came out several minutes later I followed my plan of leaving the suite in character right past the attendants. But when I stepped out of the bedroom into the living area, I discovered I was alone. Evidently they had finished their assignments while I was in the restroom and had left, believing me to be the real Mordecai in my own home.

"It didn't seem like a problem at all, though, until I tried to leave the suite. The main door was now locked, and, I realized with a start, required a key from both sides! I was locked in Mordecai's rooms until someone came to find me."

Paul was laughing now, too, even as he told the story.

"I had to stay in there for over two hours before I heard a key being turned in the lock. I stood up in front of the door, waiting. As luck would have it, it was Mordecai himself who entered the room! The only thing I could think of was to stay in character, so as Mordecai drew up in surprise at seeing me, I announced in my best impersonation, 'Hello there, Mordecai Old Chap! It's jolly good to see you!'"

All three of us were rolling in laughter at this point. Paul played it with the perfection of someone who has told this story countless times, but never gets tired of telling it any more than we got tired of hearing it.

"I thought Mordecai was going to have a heart attack!" he exclaimed. "He just stood there, staring. Finally, he backed out of the room and began calling for help. Pretty soon, there were attendants, Hall leaders, teachers and onlookers crowding into the suite. Nobody knew what to make of my little prank. Finally, it was determined that since I was technically still a student, the consequences would be relatively mild. I spent the next several weeks either in class, on supervised work duty, or confined to my room. A mark was put into my record, and my hopes for being selected for further study were all but dashed."

"However, on the day when I was released from my punishment, I was called to Mordecai's office. It seemed he had learned of the motivations behind my ill-planned shenanigans and was actually somewhat appreciative of my efforts. He had looked into my background and decided to select me as his pupil after all. 'But,' he added without a trace of humor, 'don't ever dress up like me again.'"

We had thoroughly enjoyed Paul's story, and would have normally taken its ending to be the signal for bed, but Paul. Looking thoughtful, decided to add something.

"Mary, I know you enjoy hearing stories of the Hall because you miss it very much. Sometimes I still miss it too. And I know that I didn't really leave of my own volition any more than you did. But I want you to understand that since I left, I have grown to know Jesus so much in ways I never could have if I had stayed. Although I never would have made the decision to leave on my own, now I wouldn't ever want to go back. Being on the outside for awhile has given me a better perspective. And as I think about life on the Path of Satisfying God, I think it is really a lot like my story."

Mary was staring into the fire, obviously uncomfortable with the direction our conversation had turned. So I spoke up in her place, keeping the momentum going by responding, "How's that, Paul?"

"Well, I really wanted to be a follower of Mordecai, and to be as close to him as I could. So I imitated him to a ridiculous degree. I learned everything about his appearance and mannerisms and likes and dislikes and incorporated those into myself. I was even able to fool some people. But when I came face to face with the real Mordecai, I was a ridiculous phony. And even though he eventually accepted me and helped me, he never had a desire for me to impersonate him at all.

"That's kind of like what the Hall has done with Jesus. We want to know Jesus and be his followers, so we've taken everything we know about him and copied it, even turning it into rules. For instance, we believe that Jesus has given us purpose and joy in our lives. We take that to mean that we should always feel gratitude, joy and happiness in our lives. So it became a rule that everyone should have a smile on their face all the time. At some point back before anyone can remember, somebody realized that it was too hard to make themselves smile all the time and started wearing a mask with a smile on it. Others thought it was a good idea, and followed suit. Now everybody does it, and the mask has become mandatory. Most people couldn't even tell you that the mask is related to feeling joy and purpose in living in relationship with Jesus. The rule of mask-wearing has replaced the relationship. We could identify dozens of other examples of how we have done that.

"And to make matters worse, where we don't know something about Jesus, we've just made something up. We've decided that Jesus wants everything neat and clean, so we've made rules about cleaning the path and removing stones.

"Or how about this: you know about the Tree Painters, don't you? Why do they do that? I haven't the foggiest idea! But at some point in the past someone thought that it was a way to honor and worship God. I would guess it is some sort of imitation of his act of creation, but I don't know. It may be that there were dead or dying trees on the grounds that people thought Jesus would disapprove of, so they painted them, and then just kept on going. So now we have individuals who have quite sincerely dedicated their lives to serving Jesus by painting trees every day, all day long. But the work, however sincere, has replaced the relationship with Jesus.

"What I'm trying to get at, Mary, is that stepping back from the rules and instead building a relationship with Jesus has opened my eyes to a whole new world. It's not that everything the Hall does is bad. In fact, a lot of it is very good, and most of the people there are sincerely trying to follow Jesus the only way they know how. The sad thing is that those good things could be done because they celebrate a relationship we already have with Jesus, instead of as efforts to earn that relationship apart from him. Other things we find have no purpose at all, and can just as easily be abandoned."

I thought Paul's words were profound, and it was obvious that Mary was listening intently. But she wasn't ready to drop her guard yet. She was like a scared puppy that desperately needed someone to take care of her and love her, but didn't really know who she could trust. Without a word, she stood up and went to her tent. Later, as I lay in my own tent, I thought I could hear muffled crying from her direction.

Then the day finally came that I approached camp after a day of exploring to see Jesus there with her, holding her in his arms. I stopped, giving them their privacy, and Paul came up beside me to put his arm around my shoulders. Tears were flowing freely down his face, and I joined him.

Chapter 9 – Reaching Out

Jesus came to see us almost every day for the next few weeks. He spent most of his time with Mary, but also went on walks alone with Paul or me and would sit around the campfire in the evenings telling stories, singing songs, and laughing about anything and everything. This period of time is one of my favorite memories.

We could see Mary being changed as well. Gradually, with many starts and stops, she began to embrace the freedom of life on the Path of Trusting Jesus. She was much more lighthearted, and genuinely interested in Paul's and my experiences out here in the wild, instead of just our past in the Hall. I think giving up her idolization of the Hall's way of life was the hardest for her, and it came back in unexpected ways for the longest time. Still, we could see the transformation Jesus was bringing about in her in new ways almost every day, and it was exciting to witness. We wondered if our own growth had been as dramatic in our early days of trusting Jesus. It probably was.

One evening, sitting around the fire eating S'mores, Jesus got our attention with something more serious than our normal playful banter.

"I am so excited about what is happening in each one of your lives. I'm very glad for the relationship I have with each one of you. I am also very glad for the relationship you have with one another. Do not take your friendship for granted. But I think it is time for you to move forward and take the next steps in your journey."

"And what does that look like, Jesus?" Paul asked with anticipation. I began to immediately think of new trails, new sights, and new challenges. But that wasn't exactly what Jesus had in mind.

"There are many people out there who want to know me, but are struggling to understand some of the truths you are now learning to live out."

"You want us to help others find this trail that we are on," Mary said with certainty, as though she had already known it. "I've been thinking the same thing. When I left the Hall, I discovered there were lots of people living out there, not sure where to go or what to do next. If I hadn't been in so much pain myself, I would have become friends with many of them. At the time, I just wanted to be left alone. But now that I have a better understanding of you, Jesus, I've been thinking about going back to find some of them."

Jesus smiled. "Yes, that is exactly it. It's not fair to hide the joy you've found when it could help so many others. What do you say?"

I honestly hadn't thought much about this prospect. It was true that Paul and I were able to help Mary when she was completely at the end of her rope. We became her friends when she was hurting and desperate and through that relationship Jesus was able to speak his love to her.

But that just sort of happened. We had no doubt that Jesus led us down the right trail to come across Mary that day, but we weren't looking for someone to help. We were just able to do the right thing when Jesus brought us together. I wasn't sure we were cut out for the kind of intentional campaign Jesus was talking about.

Mary began to describe what she had seen, her voice growing stronger with the passion she felt for this calling. "There are all kinds of people who have left the Hall of Good Works for whatever reason that are just stuck, just camping out there along the trail hoping something will come along and change things for them. Some of them were sent away like I was because they had rebelled or failed in some way. Some left on their own, realizing that something was wrong with the Hall, but not knowing there was anything different. They are all over out there, and perhaps we could be more intentional about helping some of them."

Finally, Paul and I agreed, although I admit I was still nervous. The next day we began to make plans, and Jesus disappeared again as he was apt to do. In the days that followed we prayed frequently for Jesus to connect us with those that he would have us to help the way that he did with Mary. And we talked about how to find the people that Mary was talking about. Of course we were going to need to go where the people were, we realized. Setting up some sort of communal tent where we were and hoping people would come find was preposterous. We decided our best opportunities would come if we spent time hiking around the Path of Satisfying God.

The first day out, we didn't see anybody. After several hours of hiking, we returned to our camp. We were dejected but still hopeful.

The second day we did the same thing, with exactly the same results. And the third. That night as we ate around the campfire we asked Mary if she was sure that there were people out here, and she assured us that there were. "But they are wary of strangers, wary of being misled again," she added.

On the fourth morning, it was raining. It was a downpour, and we were discouraged from the outset. I just wanted to stay in camp for the day and try again when the weather was better. After some discussion and prayer, and some pushing from Mary, we decided to take a short hike, just to see what we could find. The rain was coming down in sheets, and we were all three quickly soaked to the bone and quite miserable. "What are we doing out here?" I thought. "We're likely to get sick and be of no use to anyone!"

 After only about an hour, even Mary was ready to give up and turn around. We huddled up so we hear one another and discuss our options. Just then we heard cries in the distance. It sounded like people were yelling, but we couldn't make it out at all.

Without a second thought, we turned towards the sounds and started walking, hoping we could even find them through this downpour. After a few minutes of searching, we broke into a clearing to see somebody's camp. One side of their tent had fallen in the rain and water was running in the open door. That's what must have prompted the yelling. Quickly we moved to help a man and a woman we had never seen before stand the poles back up and get ropes secured so that they wouldn't fall again. We could see that there were two young children inside, huddled up for warmth. But the water had already rushed in, soaking most of the blankets beyond use.

"Do you have any firewood?" Paul yelled above the storm, looking at the man. The man pointed to a wood pile that wasn't covered at all. It would be several days before the wood would be dry enough to use. We had made sure that our wood back at our camp was secured under tarps, so Paul and Mary decided to go back to get it. I stayed to help the man secure a canopy so there would be a place to build the fire out of the rain once they got back. By the time Paul and Mary returned with loads of wood wrapped in tarps we were all shivering and cold. We got a fire going as quickly as we could with shaking fingers, then brought the children out to warm up by the fire.

Only after we were all warmer and considerably drier did we start to talk. We learned that the man's name was Peter and his wife was Sarah. Joshua was eight years old and Rebecca was only four. They professed how grateful they were for our help but seemed very standoffish all the same. Still, they couldn't very well send us out into the rain when it was our firewood they were burning, so slowly we began to talk about deeper issues.

Paul told them his story of leaving the Hall because of the rejection he felt when rumors spread. Paul's story was always a moving one, and it convinced Peter to open up about their own experiences.

"We lived in the Hall of Good Works for several years," he started, "but left almost three years ago. We just became disillusioned with the whole thing – the rules, the masks, the managers. We felt like the Hall had too much power over our lives and was coming between Jesus and us.

"Our family manager seemed to care more about how our actions made him look than he did about helping us satisfy God. The longer we stayed the more control he gained over us. He would scrutinize every little thing we did and talk about how it reflected on his reputation or how it wasn't good enough for

God. So in the end, we secretly packed our stuff and snuck away in the middle of the night."

"And so you've just camped here since that time?" Mary asked.

"Mostly," Sarah answered. "With two little children, travel is difficult. So we found this place where no one would bother us and we settled in. We do our best to satisfy God and teach the children the same, but we can't go back to that Hall. We only hope it is enough in the end."

As I listened to Peter's and Sarah's story, my heart broke for this family. These were good people, but they had been lied to over and over by people who wanted to use them for their own benefit – people who used God's name to manipulate them. I wondered if they could ever be convinced to trust Jesus again when their trust had been betrayed so badly already. But I looked over at Paul and Mary and I thought of how Jesus had overcome all of the baggage that we had brought to him, and I reminded myself that it wasn't our job to convince them, only to love them. Jesus would overcome their struggles with his love the same way he did for each of us. And in that moment, I realized why Mary had been so passionate about seeking out these people and others like them.

So I began to tell my story to this family – I was honest about my struggle with Black Water, and I told them about my time spent at the Hall of Good Works as well as how Jesus had guided me through each step of my journey until I found freedom on a different trail, the Path of Trusting God. I could tell they were very interested, but they were also wary. I was aware that this was exactly the sort of thing someone might say who was trying to manipulate them again.

Finally, Mary told her story as well. Peter and Sarah listened intently, the children now asleep in their arms. By the time the rain let up a few hours later, we had made new friends. But they were not ready to follow us to the Path of Trusting God just yet.

As the sun came out and the kids, now awake, started playing in the mud, Peter said he wanted to check on another family that camped nearby. We volunteered to go with him. It turned out that this family had weathered the storm better than Peter and Sarah, but they mentioned someone else who camped at the bottom of a ravine. We went that way next, and found two men who had seen everything they owned washed down the mountainside by a flood of water. We shared our food, some clothes, and even gave them a tent. Two of us could share until I could get a new one of my own.

These men led us to yet another family that had stayed dry in a cave but had a sick child. I don't know where she got it, but Mary had some medicine she left with them.

By the end of the day, we had met over a dozen people or families when all our traipsing around the trails had been fruitless. And all the while, Peter watched and sometimes helped as we served people who were struggling.

Finally, Peter invited us back to his camp as the sun began to go down. "After all," he said with a grin, "We've got your firewood."

It was that night around the campfire that Peter said, "I've watched you all day to see if you really are who you say you are. I thought you would try to get people to pay you back somehow for helping them, you know, by coming to work in your camp or something. I don't know. But what I saw was that you gave generously today without asking for anything in return. You even gave some of your own supplies when people needed them. I don't think the people in the Hall would have done that."

I didn't know what to say to his praise. I realized that it was true that we had done all that he said, but I hadn't thought about it like that while I was doing it. I just saw people in need and tried to help them as best I could.

Paul responded, "Jesus has given us so much, and we just want to continue giving what he has given to us. To give love and to give Jesus to people doesn't cost us – in fact it gives us as much or more back in return."

That seemed to satisfy Peter. After we turned in, he and Sarah stayed up next to the fire for a long time talking. The next morning we got up to find them breaking camp. "We want to follow you to the Path of Trusting God," they said, big grins on their faces. So off we went. After that, we stayed in contact with them, helping them on their new journey, and we also continued to help and serve new friends that we met through the others we had helped that day.

I began to feel a renewed sense of purpose knowing that I was able to help others find the same freedom in Jesus that had changed my life. It reminded me a little bit of when I had helped others find the square of Blue Sky in the Maze, although this time I was much more confident that I was actually providing people with something that would make a real difference in their lives. And I wasn't expecting payment anymore, either.

We kept up this work for a good, long time, and never had trouble finding people to help anymore. After a while though, there was a growing restlessness inside my heart. More and more, my mind turned towards memories of the Maze. Finally, I shared my feelings with Paul and Mary.

"I left a friend back in the maze," I said. "His name was Mark. We hung out in the Pools of Black Water together. The day I left, he wasn't interested at all. He saw the man who led me out and swam away from him. But now I think maybe Jesus wants me to go back and talk to him again. To see if maybe he is ready to trust Jesus now."

Paul and Mary were very encouraging. Paul added, "Of course, I'm coming with you. You're going to need me to keep you out of trouble, I'm sure." I knew what he was thinking about – the temptation of the Black Water. I didn't think it would be an issue for me, but I certainly wasn't going to become self-righteous about it. And I was relieved to know that I would have his company.

After some discussion, we all agreed that Mary would stay and continue the work we'd been doing until we Paul and I got back.

Chapter 10 – Back to the Maze

Once we had decided to go back to the Maze and find my friend Mark, I was anxious to get started. But Paul cautioned me, telling me that this experience would be different than I remembered it. "For one thing," he said, "you and I aren't going back across the Bridge over the Dark Chasm. Jesus has saved us from that, and we can't go back the way we came."

"Then how do we get there?" I asked. "I thought Jesus was the only way across."

"Oh yes," Paul said, nodding his head. "Jesus is the only Bridge. We're not going back into the Maze the way you are thinking about it. Rather, we are going to find someone who is in the Maze, and that's a different thing altogether."

"You've lost me," I say. "How do we find someone whom we know is in a place we aren't going to?"

Paul grinned at my wit, then continued, "We're going to climb Mount Rescue. Don't worry, it's just as daunting as it sounds."

I gave him a quizzical stare, and he continued, obviously enjoying himself. "As followers of Jesus, we can go where the people who aren't followers of Jesus are without entering into the Maze. You see, the Maze is a lie. It is a false perception given to people to keep them unaware that they are really slaves. God's enemy does this because he doesn't want them to know the truth. He doesn't want them to realize that they need to cross the Bridge Jesus has built. So he created this Maze to convince people that they are really on this path or that path, that they are going somewhere.

"So Jesus has made it possible for us to see the truth. We can see the Maze for what it really is. We will climb Mount Rescue and on the other side we will see the true path these people are on. We have to be on our guard, because the Maze will try to make itself seem real to us, try to convince us that we are there and it is real. We will need each other and we will need the strength and presence of Jesus to help us stay focused on the truth."

His explanation didn't really make a lot of sense to me, but I trusted that he knew what he was talking about.

Paul took us around to all of our friends to tell them what we were doing and to ask them to pray for us. Then we set off for Mount Rescue. The trip was uneventful, although we could see the Dark Abyss running adjacent to the mountain. Finally, we came up over a rise to see what the Maze really was, and it was not what I was prepared for at all.

Below us was a huge valley sloping down with high rock walls on either side. The walls were so high that they kept the valley floor in constant shadow. The lower part of the valley appeared to get steeper and steeper until it eventually came to an abrupt end over the edge of the Dark Abyss. Everything in the valley slanted downwards toward the Abyss. I couldn't believe that when I had been in the Maze myself it felt like I was going uphill all the time, when really I was going down. It was all designed to lead people downward toward their eventual demise.

As we peered down into the valley from above, it occurred to me that there might be some connection to the fact that this is a valley of sorts while people in the Maze always hoped of making it to the Beautiful Valley. But of course there was no Beautiful Valley, only a Valley of Death.

Paul and I made our way down to the valley floor in silence. The farther we descended, the darker and colder in became, and it struck me how different it was from when I found the Maze hot and stuffy. Once we reached the bottom, we began to come across people. Every one of them was carrying a huge, heavy backpack on their backs. I remembered that when I had worn that backpack I had understood that it was full of all the baggage from my life. But I didn't remember it being as heavy and crippling as the ones these people were wearing.

I took notice of a particular woman as I passed her. She was almost doubled over with the weight of her pack, with a look of pain on her face. Instinctively, I reached out to help her as she careened to one side only to feel a sting as she slapped my hand away.

"What do you think you are doing?" she demanded.

I drew back, uncertain, then said, "I just wanted to help you with your pack..."

"Do I look like I need help?" she spat even more vehemently. Obviously she thought the answer was "no," but from my perspective she could hardly stand up!

"Um...I'm sorry...I didn't mean..." I stumbled.

She turned her back on me, almost hitting me with the pack, and shuffled off down the street.

Paul chuckled behind me. "People here don't see the same reality that you see."

"Apparently," I sighed. "I'll have to be more careful."

We kept walking deeper and deeper into the valley. Suddenly, I caught a glimpse of a strange shadow out of the corner of my eye, but when I turned my head it was gone. I wouldn't have thought much of it, except that it happened again. And again.

I said something to Paul, and he said he had noticed the same thing. He didn't know what it was either, and I commented that I never saw anything like it when I lived in the Maze.

Then we turned a corner to see a man pushing himself up against a large rock in a strange way. He was facing the rock and has his arms and legs spread wide, all the while talking to himself. We moved closer so that we could hear him, but it sounded like pure gibberish. I stopped, not sure if I wanted to engage the man or just run the other way. That's when I saw the shadow again, this time over the disturbed man's shoulder. It quickly disappeared behind him, then popped out above the other shoulder before disappearing again. I froze, shocked by what I was seeing and unable to reconcile it in my mind.

Paul was only slightly less shaken than I was, but he took a step closer and announced, "Excuse me sir, but can we talk to you?"

The man spun around, noticing us for the first time. "Who are you? Can't you see I'm teaching these people how to mountain climb? You could have scared me into falling!"

What was he talking about? I felt like I was three steps behind as Paul went with what the man was saying and continued the conversation.

"We're sorry to interrupt," Paul said with a slight bow. "But we wondered if you could help us?"

"Help you? What does this look like, some sort of charity? This is a place of business. Next time make an appointment with my receptionist."

Paul remained nonplussed. "We'll do that. But since we're here, I wondered if you could answer a question for me?"

"Make it quick," the man retorted. "I've got a class to teach."

It occurred to me with a start that this man might not actually be crazy. From my viewpoint, there was certainly no mountain, no receptionist and no class. But as my mind played catch up with the strange encounter, I realized that perhaps these things were exactly what he was experiencing inside the Maze! In other words, it might not have been in his head, but rather the lie of the Maze that made him believe he was a successful climbing instructor.

Paul asked, "Do you know what that strange shadow is that keeps popping up behind you?"

The man looked perplexed, and immediately became even more defensive than before. "What are you talking about? Are you insane? I'm calling security."

"No need for that," Paul replied calmly. "We'll go. Thank you for your time."

We moved away from the man, who immediately went back to muttering to himself. Paul turned to me, "I think I know what the shadows are. I think they are the lies the Maze tells people to give their lives false meaning. I think they are demons."

"Demons?" I balked.

Paul answered, "Yes. It's obvious that there is a conscious design to this place, that there is an intentional plan to the lies these people believe. It's going to be hard to break through the lies for some people."

I argued, "But when the man came and found me, I was sure that he was telling the truth and that I needed his help. Shouldn't we be able to expect the same from others who are here?"

"Not necessarily," Paul replied, "You were already aware that you were in trouble. You knew the Black Water was hurting you, even though you didn't know how to break away. You were aware at least in part that the Maze was a lie. For many people, that simply isn't true. For them, they are doing as well at living life here as I thought I was living in the Hall of Good Works."

I could see what Paul meant, and it filled me with despair. How could we ever hope to communicate with any of these people? How could we expect to find Mark, and what would I say to him if I did find him?

We walked on in silence, both wrapped in our own thoughts. Walls appeared on both sides of us as we moved deeper into the Maze, getting taller as we went, up to twenty feet high. Soon it seemed like we were going around in circles, and I realized with a start that I had no idea which we way we had come from. I should have been paying better attention to my surroundings. I hoped Paul knows where we were, because I was totally turned around..."Paul? Paul?"

Suddenly I realized that Paul was no longer beside me! Where was he? How long had he been gone? I turned around and quickly walked back the way I had come. "Paul! Paul!" I cried out, becoming frantic.

Then a man approached me and I stopped, surprised by his appearance. He was clean-cut with a stylish haircut and was wearing a pin-striped suit and tie. He immediately struck me as someone who didn't belong here in the Maze, someone who was better than this place. Although I knew that I didn't belong here either, at least not anymore, I was suddenly filled with embarrassment at having been found here.

"He left you, didn't he?" the man asked.

"What? Who?" I stammered, not understanding.

"Your companion," he replied calmly. "Paul. He left you here while he went back out of the Maze."

"No, he wouldn't do that," I responded dumbly.

"Then where is he?" the man asked. "You're all alone. And it's just as well, you know. You never should have left in the first place. You belong here, where you can find a real purpose. And where you can enjoy the refreshing Black Pools free of guilt and shame."

I hesitated. His words felt right in my mind, yet wrong at the same time. I couldn't quite put my finger on what was happening to me, like I was groggy or just waking up. "Who are you?" I blurted.

"A friend," he replied. "Someone who wants to help you find your true path. Out there you were always a loser, trying to stop what your heart knew you were meant for, just because that man wanted you to. He doesn't really love you, you know. He's just using you."

"Man? Paul?" I just couldn't quite follow this strange man's logic, but part of me desperately wanted to. He seemed like he held some sort of wisdom I was lacking.

"No, not Paul. He's just as much a victim as you are. I mean the other man, the one who took you away from the Maze in the first place. The one who is manipulating you for his own gain."

Suddenly, something clicked into place. "You mean Jesus?" I asked incredulously. The man nodded seriously, but with a slight look of pain on his face. That's when my mind came awake again and suddenly I could see straight through his lies. I knew Jesus, and nothing this man could say was ever going to change that. He almost convinced me that I didn't deserve to be outside the Maze. He almost had me believing once again that the Black Water was refreshing. He might even have been able to convince me that Paul had abandoned me. But this last trick was too much- he would never convince me of that Jesus didn't love me!

"Get away from me!" I cried, backing up and waving my arms erratically in front of me, trying to block the man from my presence somehow. Suddenly everything changed before my eyes. The walls around me are disappeared, and and I could see the valley around me once again. The man was gone too, and in his place stood Paul, looking at me hard.

"Are you alright?" he asked, concern mirrored in his eyes.

"I think so. That man..."

But Paul interrupted, "That wasn't a man. You had one of those shadows flying around you. But now it's gone."

"That was scary," I said. "What he was saying seemed so real that I almost went with him. And all of these people live like this all the time! We have to help them!"

"We will," Paul said. "At least the ones we can. When you're up to it, let's keep going."

So we kept walking. We tried to talk to some people, while others we could tell were caught up too much in their own shadowy lies to even understand us properly, like the man trying to climb the rock. It was very discouraging.

Then I saw someone I recognized! It was the girl I met briefly when I first entered the maze. She was the one who stood in line with me at the Information desk, and who first told me about the Beautiful Valley. She looked older than she had then, and obviously weighed down more by her pack. She looked intently around her as she walked, frequently glancing down at a crumpled piece of paper in her hands.

"Hello," I called out. She stopped, turning towards me.

"Hello," she answered, friendly but obviously not recognizing me.

"I don't know if you remember me," I said, walking up to her, "but we met a long time ago, in line at the Information Desk."

"Oh, yeah, I remember you," she said. "You look different now though."

"Yeah, a lot older I'm sure."

"No," she shook her head. "That's not it. You look...lighter somehow. And more self-aware."

"Oh, yeah," I said, not sure how to proceed. "I think that's because I met Jesus, and he took my burdens away."

"Well I'm glad that worked out for you," she replied. "Jesus is a little too restrictive for me, you know."

"So what are you doing?" I asked.

"Oh, I'm trying to find the Beautiful Valley. I've got a map now." She held out the piece of paper. To me it looked completely blank, but I knew that was an argument I wouldn't be able to win.

"There is no Beautiful Valley," I said instead. She stared at me with disbelief, but I plowed on. "There is only one way out of this Maze, and it's through Jesus, not through the Beautiful Valley."

"See," she responded knowingly. "That's why I say Jesus is too restrictive. How can there be only one way, when there are all these different paths everywhere? I'm sure Jesus has been a good path for you to be on, but that doesn't mean my path isn't just as good."

"But don't you see," I argued. "There aren't really a bunch of paths. This Maze is only taking you in one direction, towards the Dark Abyss."

"That's ridiculous," she retorted, holding out her piece of paper. "This shows we are nowhere near the Dark Abyss. Besides, I've decided I don't even believe in that old Abyss mythology. That's just a fairy tale told to scare children. And to fool people like you," she added.

"But I've seen it," I said, growing desperate. "I've crossed over it, on the Bridge Jesus built."

"That may be what you thought you saw," she replied matter-of-factly, "But that doesn't mean it was real. I only believe what I can see with my own two eyes."

"But that's the lie," I said, exasperated. Paul put a hand on my shoulder and whispered, "You can't argue with her. She can't see it. You can only show her what Jesus means to you."

I nodded and tried to start again. "Let me tell you my story..."

But she put up a hand to stop me. "I don't really have time for this, and I don't want to be preached at. I've got to go. It was nice to see you again. I'm glad you're doing so well, really."

And off she went. Only we could still see her. She turned and walked a few feet one way, then turned and walked a few feet the other way. Paul and I stood and watched, and even after several minutes she was still standing only a few feet away from us. Yet she was totally oblivious to our presence once again and intently staring at her crumpled piece of paper.

I felt even more discouraged, but Paul reminded me that Jesus had sent us here to find Mark. It didn't mean there couldn't be other opportunities, but that was the mission we were on.

So we moved on, looking in every direction for some clue that could lead us to Mark. Eventually our path carried us to the Black Pool. Immediately I was shocked to see what it looked like from my new perspective. Instead of lots of pools scattered around the Maze, there was really only one giant pit in the middle of a clearing. Black sludge came up out of the ground, smelling like a sewer. Hundreds, maybe thousands of people frolicked in it, the sludge running down their faces, over their eyes, into their open mouths as they laughed out loud. It was deplorable. I was filled with disgust, contempt and pity all at the same time.

Then I noticed one of the shadows circling what looked like a pipe with a valve coming up out of the middle of the pit. The valve turned and the sludge disappeared into the ground. All the people started to walk away in all directions. Only when the water level was low enough, I could see that they all wore shackles around their ankles, attached to chains leading back to the pipe. When they reached the end of the chain, they just stopped, standing bewildered.

After a few minutes, the shadow turned the valve again and up came the sludge. The people all ran back to it and jumped in, laughing and happy once again.

"It's horrible," I uttered through clenched teeth. How could these people live like this? How could I have once lived like this? I was ready to run away, leave the valley, forget all about Mark, and spend the rest of my life in my comfortable little camp site with the pool and the clay and my friends.

But Paul stepped forward, putting his arm around my shoulders. "Yes it is. But you have to look past the sludge, past the smell, and see that those are people. They have been lied to, enslaved, and abused. But they are people, and Jesus loves them just as much as he loves you and me. But if you go over there and show them how disgusted you are, they will never listen. You have to go over there and show them you love them too."

I understood what Paul was telling me. I thought back to when the man came and rescued me from this nightmare; that he showed no concern about the smell or appearance, that he had even touched me. That had been impressive even when I had just thought it was Black Water, not sewer sludge.

With that, I took a deep breath and made my way down to the edge of the pit, an embankment falling away before me where the sludge reached when it was at its highest, and scanned the faces before me. Finally I saw him - Mark. There he was, wallowing in the sludge. Only he wasn't laughing or enjoying the sludge like many of the people around him. He just sort of sat there. I waited until the sludge level dropped down again, and Mark started to walk away, the chains holding him back. Taking a swig from my water bottle, I stepped forward and slid down the embankment into the pit. I approached the spot where he was standing motionless, the chain taut behind him, tethering him mercilessly to the pipe.

"Mark," I called out.

He seemed to wake up and turned towards me immediately, recognizing me as his old friend. "Where have you been?" he asked, not missing a beat. "Man, you've missed all kinds of excitement around here! It's been crazy good. C'mon and help me find another pool. Hey, what happened to your pack?"

"Mark, things have changed for me now. I know I haven't really missed any excitement here, because everything always stays the same. But I've been set free from all this, and from my

baggage, by Jesus. I did miss you, though. That's why I'm here.
"

 I briefly told Mark my story, promising him that Jesus could rescue him too. Once I reached the end, I asked, "Would you like to come with me to meet Jesus?"

Mark nodded, emotional and unable to speak. He took a step towards me, but just then the sludge started to rise again. Suddenly the chain around his ankle tightened and began to retract, pulling him back towards the sludge. My mind raced. How could I free him from the chain? I must have been chained up like that too, once. What did the man who came to me do to set me free? Mark was being dragged backward, as I stood helplessly. I took a step back to keep my own feet from being covered by the sludge, then another. It was almost up to Mark's waist again. He looked desperately at me, his eyes wide, but I could tell that he couldn't do anything to help himself. He would be covered again in just a few seconds.

Then it hit me. The touch. I jumped forward, ignoring the sludge that was coming up over my ankles, and ran to Mark as fast as I could, throwing my arms around him. Immediately the shackles fell off and pulled back into the sludge. The sludge itself seemed to shrink away from us, opening up a path back out of the pit. Mark was free as he clung to me.

Paul appeared at the edge of the pit, reaching down as far as he could. Mark reached up, and Paul pulled him up. I clamber out of the pit as well, and we all stand staring at each other, wide-eyed.

 "Let's get out of here," I said. "Which way?"

"Towards the Abyss," Paul said.

I looked at him questioningly. But Paul said simply, "Jesus will be there."

We led Mark toward the edge of the Abyss. To us it seemed like a straight walk across the valley floor, but Mark seems confused. He looked all around, sometimes turning one way or the other but always returning to follow us. And more than once I saw him staring back in the direction of the pit.

Then we approached the edge of the Abyss, and sure enough, there was Jesus with a huge smile on his face. As we approached, he wrapped his arms around Mark, drawing him in. Paul and I stepped back.

"OK," Paul said, breathing out. "Now I suggest we get back down to our side to meet Mark before he makes another poor choice in choosing a path."

I agreed wholeheartedly.

Chapter 11 – Seeking Blue Sky

"I want to invite the four of you to go on an adventure," Jesus announced. We were immediately interested, so he continued. "I am just thrilled that the four of you have become such good friends, and that you see your relationship with each other is an extension of your relationship with me. I just love how you help each other to trust me more, especially as Mark has been going through such an important transition. I am inviting the four of you to make a journey together that will strengthen and deepen your relationship even more, and, I think, strengthen your relationship with me in the process."

It had been four months since Mark left the Maze and followed Jesus over the Bridge. I was amazed at how quickly Mark transitioned to living on the Path of Trusting Jesus. When Paul and I met him after his encounter with Jesus, he was more than willing to join us and forgo the Path of Satisfying God altogether. He joined our camp, pitched in wherever he could in our work to help others, and quickly became an integral part of our community. Of course, Jesus came and spent long periods of time with him, until finally calling all of us together for his announcement.

"Where are we going?" Mary asked, obviously ready to go.

Jesus smiled and looked at me. "I know that the mountains and that the sky has a special significance for you. I know of a peak high in the mountains where the sky opens up all around you, where you can see farther than you ever thought possible. A place where the clouds are beneath you and the blue vastness above you seems like it will never stop. It's a place where the rocks sing my father's name in praise, echoing endlessly off one another, and you can feel my heartbeat in the beauty all around you. It's a place that is very special to me."

Jesus' voice rises with excitement then softens to almost a whisper as he describes the awe and holiness of the destination he has chosen for us. All four of us are instantly anxious to set out for such a wonder.

"I need to warn you, though," Jesus added with seriousness in his voice. "This trail is not for the faint of heart. There will be many hardships along the way. There will be temptations that will call out to each one of you. You will all four need the others in order to make it. In fact, I would never send just one of you, or even two. This journey is something special for all of you."

I felt a certain pride in the strength of our relationship as I looked from Mary's face to Paul's, then over to Mark's, and I think Mary felt the same. Mark looked nervous, and Paul was surprisingly less enthusiastic.

"Before we get too excited," he said, spreading his arms downward as if to calm us down, "I would like to know more about these hardships and temptations. Jesus, why would you send us somewhere that you know holds temptations for us?"

"Because I have something greater for you in your life than even this," Jesus replied, motioning to our camp. "There are certainly times in life when it is good to stop and rest and just be still, allowing your soul to abide in me in the calmness of the day. You have also taken great advantage of the opportunities I have given you to help others nearby. But there are also times when you need to move forward, into new territories and on new adventures, in order to find more and more of me. If you stay still too long, you can become complacent. Quite frankly, you've been here long enough."

"But what if the temptation is too much for us?" Paul questioned, still not convinced. "What if one of us fails? What if we fail each other?"

"That is indeed a risk," Jesus agreed. Let's think about it. Why don't you tell me, 'What if you fail'?"

Paul seemed taken aback, and fell silent in contemplation. Mary, too, didn't look like she knew how to answer this question. So I spoke up.

"As one with plenty of experience in this area," I started, trying to sound jovial, "I think I can answer that question." Looking at my friends, I continued, "Failure is certainly no fun, but it isn't the end of the world. I would never choose sin as a way to know Jesus better, but I can tell you that Jesus has never abandoned me because of my sinful choices. He has always been there to pick me up, loving me when I'm failing just as much as he does when I'm trusting him. So the answer to your question is, 'we trust in Jesus' grace and we press on'." I turned back to Jesus, "Am I right, Jesus?"

Jesus smiled, "Spoken like a man with experience." We all laughed.

We spent the next day packing for the trip. We also took down our camp, stowing things we didn't want to take with us under a nearby tree, thinking we would come back this way after our journey. We were surprised to see just how much stuff we had accumulated during the time we had stayed there. Since he had been here the shortest period of time, Mark was the one with the least amount of stuff. He was packed and ready to go by midmorning, and spent the rest of the day helping others get ready.

The only thing I did not pack away was the sculpture I had made of Jesus and I in the embrace. I left it out as a landmark and a witness to any other travelers who might come this way. I had always enjoyed looking at the sculpture because of how it reminded me of my relationship with Jesus. It made me sad to leave it behind, but I reminded myself that I had the real Jesus with me all the time.

On the second morning after receiving the challenge from Jesus, we set out. Of course, Jesus didn't give us a map. He never did. He had told us how to find the trailhead, and that was always enough for him. I guess he didn't ever want us to think we could find our way on our own, even with a map from him.

Jesus was completely right about this trail. The terrain was difficult, and we needed each other to help one another in various ways. One person could never manage to climb this mountain alone.

The path was often so faint that it was hard to distinguish it from our surroundings, and more than once we had to backtrack when what we thought was the trail disappeared on us. I never would have guessed it, but Mark turned out to be the expert at discerning the true path. When we came upon a particularly rocky area where no signs of previous travelers could be seen, Mark confidently steered us up and down over the rocks until we arrived on the other side, exactly where the obvious trail continued on. Dumbfounded, I asked him how he knew.

"If you pay close attention, you can sense the movements of Jesus," he replied, taking a drink from his water bottle. "I don't know how else to explain it, but I could almost see the outline of him climbing over the rocks ahead of us. I just stepped where I saw him step."

On our second day, we came to a place where the path had been washed away, leaving a drop-off with a rock wall on one side. The path led away up the mountain on the other side, so we knew we hadn't made a wrong turn. Mark was discouraged as he looked anxiously around. "I don't see any sign of the path Jesus took. This must have happened since he was here. Now it looks like the whole mountain is blocked. I think we'll have to go back."

"Wait," Mary interrupted. "I think Jesus knew exactly what we would find. I think he intends for us to overcome even this obstacle, even if it isn't as clear as it has been before."

"What do you suggest?" I asked.

"Give me your rope," she responded. I dug it out of my knapsack as she took a big drink from her water bottle. Then she tied one end of the rope around her waist and handed me the other end. "Don't let me fall," she stated simply. Then, with nimbleness I never would have guessed she had, she shimmied up over the rocks and tied a rope to the other side! I tied off my end and Paul, Mark and I were able to cross using the rope for balance against the rocks.

"How do I get my rope back?" I wondered aloud.

"Leave it," Mary called out over her shoulder as she led the way up the trail. "We'll need it when we come back. Besides, someone else might come along that will need it too."

The rest of us followed her on up the trail, encouraging her and congratulating her on her prowess. Paul nicknamed her the "Mountain Queen" and we all laughed.

It wasn't long before we came to another obstacle, however. This time, heavy rocks had fallen and blocked the path. "Got your muscles on?" Paul asked me. They were too heavy for Mary, but Paul, Mark and I were strong enough to move them. It was heavy work, and by the time we had a path cleared we were all tired and sweating.

By the third day, I felt like we had a handle on what this trail was all about. We had come to several physical obstacles and each of us had been able to help the others. As we broke camp that morning, I was enthused by the thought of more such challenges ahead of us. What would this day bring? A river to cross? A cliff to climb? Whatever it was, I was confident that we could overcome it together. I was soon to learn, though, that physical obstacles were not the real test involved in climbing this mountain.

We walked without incident until late in the morning, as the sun began to beat down on our heads. There were no markers to tell us how far we had come, how far we had yet to go, or what we were about to find. We came up over a rise and stopped, looking down into a valley spread out below us, open on three sides and ending abruptly at a cliff wall on the fourth. The valley held the most unexpected thing I could have ever thought of – a carnival! There were brightly colored tents, rides, a Ferris wheel, and people everywhere! Even the smell of popcorn and smoked meats wafted up into our nostrils.

I'm not sure how long we stood there, staring speechless into the strange valley below us. Finally, Paul brought us out of our shocked silence with the wisest words I think he's ever said, "I think we'd best just go around." If only we had heeded those words immediately.

But before we could really register what he was saying, a short, little bald man came scampering up to us excitedly. "Welcome! Welcome!" he shouted excitedly, hugging each of us before we even realized what was going on. "We're so glad you made it! Welcome to Paradise!"

"Paradise?" Mary asked quizzically. "What's that?"

The man stood up as tall as he could and gestured down to the valley with outstretched arms. "Why, Paradise is this!" He exclaimed. "This is Paradise!"

"It isn't what I expected Paradise to look like at all," I blurted. "What is this place doing here?"

The man shrunk back, but quickly recovered and stretched upwards once again. "Oh, but this is Paradise, my young friend. This valley has everything you could ever possibly want. It is Heaven on Earth. Utopia. Paradise. If you don't believe me yet, you certainly will. Just give it a try for a couple of hours and I guarantee you'll be singing its praises too!"

"And if we aren't?" Paul scowled.

"I have no fear of that," the little man shrugged. "But if you aren't satisfied, then you are always welcome to head back down the trail the way you came. There's nothing and nobody stopping you."

"Back down?" Mark asked, motioning to the peak that still rose above us across the valley. "But we want to keep going, up the trail to the top of the mountain."

"My dear young friend," the little man laughed. "You've made it! This is it! The end of the trail. This is as close to the top of the mountain as you can physically get. This is where Jesus wanted you to come! Paradise, in a beautiful valley setting!"

Where had I heard that phrase before? Warning bells went off in my head, but I couldn't quite put it together. Mary was smiling, happy to think we had reached our destination. Paul didn't seem convinced, but he did lower his knapsack off his shoulders and take a step towards the valley.

"Excellent!" exclaimed our new little friend. "Make yourselves at home. Explore the valley. I'm sure you will all find something that fulfills all that you desire. Welcome! Welcome!"

"Now hang on a minute!" Paul argued. "I admit I didn't know what to expect from the trail's end. But I know it doesn't include Black Water! I know enough to stay away from any place like that! And I'm not sure what that building down there is all about either! But there's something really fishy about what you're telling us!"

"Where do you see Black Water?" I asked in confusion, scanning the valley but not seeing anything so sinister.

"What building, Paul?" asked Mary. "Are you talking about one of the tents?"

Paul looked at us incredulously. "What do you mean, 'where do you see Black Water?' Where don't I see Black Water? It's everywhere! And there's only one building down there that I can see. It looks like the Hall of Good Works, only smaller."

We all looked at each other in confusion. It was obvious that Paul was seeing something completely different than the rest of us. But before we could discuss it further, the little man jumped back in. "I assure you, Sir, that there is no Black Water here. I have heard of people thinking that's what they see from a distance, however. Something about the reflection of the sun off the mountains, I have no doubt. But everything here is wholesome and fun. Just wait until you get closer, and you'll see."

"Closer? I don't want to get any closer. Can't you smell the stench?"

"It smells like turkey legs and cotton candy to me," said Mark eagerly.

"I'm not sure what you're seeing, Paul, but it's not what the rest of us see. We see a carnival full of people having fun," Mary added.

"Your friend is right," urged the little man. "This is exactly what you've been looking for! And I assure you, if there is anything here that reminds you of Black Water, it's definitely not like the Black Water you're thinking of down below. We would never let something like that in here, because we know there are such serious consequences connected to the Black Water. Everything in Paradise is wholesome and good. There are pools of water to swim in, surely, but this is water that Jesus is OK with. It won't hurt you. Jesus knows that there are legitimate needs that people are trying to meet with Black Water. It's just unfortunate that in meeting those needs there are so many negative side effects too. This water allows you to meet those needs without the side effects."

To me, his words just didn't add up. First, he claimed there is no Black Water. Then there might be something like Black Water, but different. So which one was it? Could there be something like Black Water that didn't come with all the negative consequences? Wouldn't it be perfect to be able to indulge in those things I had thought of as taboo only to find them fulfilling instead of damning? Wouldn't it be just like Jesus to give us exactly what we were looking for all along? Maybe this little man was right. Maybe not *all* Water was dangerous. Maybe it was only Black Water down below.

"Now hold on guys," Paul said cautiously. "I'm not so sure about this."

"I'm not either," I replied. "But I don't think we're going to be able to figure it out unless we at least go down and look around. If there is Black Water, we'll turn around and leave right away."

"Besides," Mark added, "if this really is the trail's end, there must be something here Jesus wants us to find. And I think it starts with a feast!"

That settled it, although looking back I can certainly see how we were only justifying out loud what we all wanted in our hearts already. We should have trusted Paul and stayed away. We failed each other that day by quietly giving each other permission to do what we each knew was really leading us away from Jesus.

But without another word, we all made our way down into the valley. We soon agreed to split up and look around, then meet back together an hour later. We agreed we wouldn't do anything, just look around and investigate.

If any of the others made it back to the rendezvous point an hour later, I don't know about it. Because I wasn't there either.

Chapter 12 – Paradise

I decided to skirt the outer edge of the encampment, wanting to see what was going on without fully engaging. Here there were dozens of individual camping tents crowded haphazardly around the valley floor, pushed up tightly against a stream that formed a natural boundary to the settlement.   It seemed to me that little to no thought had been put into organization, but rather newcomers had found any space large enough for a tent between the other tents and claimed it as their own. The result was a chaotic confusion of campsites facing all directions with no clear walkways between them. I had to navigate my way by weaving around and between tents, clotheslines, fire pits and piles of trash in order to move forward.

The place seemed practically deserted, and the few people that were visible in the encampment all appeared to be sleeping. I presumed most people must be spending their day enjoying the amenities of the valley. Nobody notices as I walked by, so I pressed on.

After fifteen minutes or so of zigzagging through the camp, I emerged on the far side. The stream was rougher here, rushing over the rocks of a much steeper incline. That must be the reason no one is camped in this area, I thought. I turned towards the interior of the valley with its inviting colors and sounds, and started walking that way, figuring there was nothing I was going to learn until I did so.

Movement caught the corner of my eye, and I turned back to my right, looking up. There was the unmistakable figure of a woman up in a tree, peering through binoculars towards the center of the valley. She was intent on what she was doing and obviously hadn't noticed me yet, and I considered walking back the other way. After a few seconds of mental debate, I instead walked towards the tree. I stopped about twenty feet away and called out, "Hello up there!"

The woman jumped, obviously startled. For a moment I was afraid she would fall out of the tree, but then she regained her grip on the large branch she was perched on and looked down at me with a mixture of irritation and embarrassment.

"What do you want?" she called down.

"Well, I was just walking by and saw you up there, and I wondered what you are doing," I called back, moving a few feet closer to the tree.

"I'm looking for someone," she responded, still sounded irritated. "Down there, in the valley."

"So why don't you just go down there and look around?" I asked curiously. "It's not that big of a place. You should be able to find them easily enough."

"You're new here, aren't you?" she asked, although she didn't wait for an answer. "Give me a second. I'm coming down."

I watched with mild interest as she slowly and clumsily climbed out of the tree. I thought more than once that she would fall as she stretched her feet down, trying to find the next foothold. Finally, she slid down the last three feet of the trunk and turned towards me, her clothes and hair in disarray and visible scratches on her arms and face.

She walked towards me, stopping a few feet away. "You haven't been down into the valley, have you?" she asked, picking up her last thought where she had left off.

"I just got here. I was just about to head down there when I saw you in the tree. Why? What's going on?"

"Well, don't," she said, looking stern. "Very few people who go into the valley ever come back. At least not for long."

I hoped she was being overdramatic, but since I already had concerns about this place her words filled me with a sense of foreboding.

"Why not?" I asked, almost afraid to hear the answer.

"Because they don't want to. Come on. Let's find a place to sit down."

She led me back into the sea of tents and finally stopped in front of one of them, indiscernible from the rest. A lone folding chair sat in front of a cold fire pit, and the woman briefly ducked into the tent and emerged with another one. We sat down, and I thought to introduce myself before continuing the conversation.

"I'm Rachel," she said, shaking my hand. "I came here five months ago with my family – my husband James and my two teenage sons. At least I think it was five months ago – time is hard to measure here. At first, we were all excited about this place. It seemed like exactly what we were looking for. We set up camp the first evening, as close to the river as we could find a place, and it struck us as odd even then how few people there were for so many tents. The next morning we all walked into the carnival together.

"I'm not sure exactly what I was expecting, but it certainly didn't do justice to what we encountered. We were met with lively music, entertaining games, delicious food and exciting rides as soon as we approached. The fun seemed never-ending. And the best part was that everything seemed clean and wholesome, with Jesus' endorsement on everything."

"What do you mean?" I asked. "Did you see Jesus here?"

"Of course not," she exclaimed, crossing her arms. "But his name is used everywhere. All the music is about him. The games have his picture on their posters. Everybody talks like they know him, nobody uses harsh or judgmental language, and nobody is caught up in any negative vices. It's like a whole different culture than anything we've experienced before. So of course we were thrilled. It was exactly the kind of environment we wanted to raise our sons in. We sent our kids off to have fun, and we did the same. At the end of the day, we were supposed to meet back here at the camp. My husband and I came back, but there was no sign of the kids. The strangest part though, was that our camp looked like no one had been in it for weeks. The food we had stored was all stale or moldy. There was a layer of dust on our sleeping bags. We began to wonder if we had been gone for longer than a day. What if the kids had come back, but we were the ones who were missing?

"So my husband went back to find them, and I stayed here in case they came back on their own. Only they never did. And neither did my husband.

"I was scared, so I started to pray. That's what we should have done in the first place. I prayed for my family's safety, and I prayed that I could find them. It was while I was praying that I felt like I needed to stay away from the stream back there. I had been relying on it for all my water. Instead, I dug out my water bottle from Jesus and started using it exclusively. Then I decided it was time to go find my family. That was three months ago, I think."

She paused, obviously coming to the part of her story she didn't want to speak out loud. She unclipped her water bottle from her belt and took a drink, then plowed forward.

"This time when I approached the carnival, it was all different. I could still hear the joyful music and see all of the happy people, but the games and activities were different. Instead of carnival attractions, there were just pools of Black Water. Do you know about Black Water?" she asked me, looking intently into my face.

"Yes," I said, alarmed. "I know about Black Water."

"Good. Then you know what kind of a place I'm talking about. I started searching every face I saw, and finally I found my younger son, Peter. I was so happy to see him, and ran up to him, but he acted like nothing was wrong. He acted like we had been together the whole time, instead of separated for months. I tried to get him to come with me, but he kept saying, 'In a minute, Mom,' or 'You go on, I'll catch up.'

"Eventually, I had to leave him there, hoping I could find my husband and he could help. And I did find my husband, in another pool, but he acted just the same. I couldn't get him to come with me at all. Then I went back to where Peter had been, but he was gone. I came back to camp, hoping to find him here, but he wasn't here either.

"I've been back to the valley several times and talked with both of them over and over, but to no avail. They always act like everything is normal and it's a great day at the carnival. And," she paused, "I've never found my older son, Jacob. Not even once."

She started to weep, and I waited, not knowing what to say. I was growing very anxious for my friends, unsure what trouble they might be in.

After several minutes, she calmed down and stated, "So that's my story. I was up in that tree hoping to see what my family was doing, hoping to see some clue as to how to break through to them. And hoping to find Jacob." She looked intently at me and added, "So that's why you need to stay away from the Valley. Don't go there."

"Actually," I said, "that's why I have to go there. I have friends there, and I have to find them."

"It won't do you any good," Rachel moaned. "If they're already in the Black Water, they won't listen to you."

"I have to try."

Another long pause, and Rachel said, "Then I'm coming with you."

"You don't have to do that."

"I want to. Maybe I can talk with my family again. And maybe I can help someone else too. Do you know what you're going to say?"

"Not really," I admitted. "But you said drinking from your water bottle helped. Where are your husband's and sons' water bottles?"

"In the tent," she said, and her eyes brightened. She disappeared inside and emerged a couple of minutes later with three more water bottles. Clipping them to the back of her belt, she said, "OK, I'm ready."

We walked towards the carnival, unintentionally moving slower and slower, and taking frequent swigs from our own water bottles. I wasn't sure how to locate any of my friends, and just hoped we would be able to spot them in the crowds. But to my surprise, we found Mark at the very first Black Water Pool we came to. He had stripped off his socks and shoes and rolled up his pant legs, but was just sitting on the ground, staring out at the water.

"Mark!" I called out, and he turned around with a start.

"Man, am I glad to see you!" he exclaimed, jumping to his feet and throwing his arms around me. Once he pulled back, he looked inquisitively over at Rachel.

"This is Rachel," I announced by way of introduction, "A friend. Her husband and sons are here in the Valley and we're hoping to bring them out."

Mark reached out his hand and gave her a warm handshake, adding, "Glad to meet you. I'm Mark."

We sat down on the grass and I briefly outlined my adventure meeting Rachel . Once I was done, I motioned to Mark's bare feet and remarked, "You seem dry enough."

Mark looked over towards the Black Water and said, "I just couldn't do it. A part of me had every intention of jumping right in, while another part of me was already filled with shame and disgust at myself for even thinking about it. I went back and forth, because I couldn't see any way out. I thought that I had to do it, even though I didn't really want to. I could hear this voice in my head telling me that this was all I was good for, and I was just pretending if I tried to do anything else. I was really twisted up inside. So then I thought maybe I would just put my feet in a little bit, and I took off my shoes and socks, but then I couldn't even do that. So I just sat down here. The strange thing is that I know I made the right choice in the end, but I felt like I was giving up somehow."

"But how did you know it was Black Water and not some carnival game?" Rachel asked.

"I think I always knew, I just didn't want to admit it. When we first saw the Valley from a distance, it looked like a carnival to me, but it just didn't look quite right, you know? Like it was fading around the edges, I guess. So when Paul said that he saw Black Water, I knew it must be true. I just didn't want it to be true. Then, after we decided to split up and explore, I started staring intently at everything, trying to see past what didn't look right. The more I stared, the more it looked like Black Water pools, until finally that's all I could see. But instead of being excited that I could see the truth, it just filled me with dismay."

"So what kept you from jumping in?" I asked. "You know that I know what a temptation it can be, and you haven't been out of the Maze that long."

"I just kept thinking about what I knew about Jesus and what I knew about Black Water. The man we met at the mouth of the valley suggested that some Black Water would be okay while other Black Water would be bad, or at least that's what I thought he was saying. But I never thought that what was so deadly about Black Water in the first place was simply that it was inherently bad in and of itself. I thought it was because it was a replacement for trusting Jesus. If that's true, then even pure, clean water could be harmful if we rely on it instead of Jesus. I don't know. I could be wrong."

I just stared at my friend for a long time, amazed at his insight. I had never thought about it quite like that, but I was suddenly sure he was right. Jesus would never approve of Black Water in one place over Black Water in another, because he wanted us to rely on him no matter where we were. Any Paradise that Jesus designed would be built around our relationship with him, not substitutes, even if they were wholesome.

"By pure, clean water I think you mean the river that feeds this Valley," said Rachel. "It seems like such an abundant source that my family and others all left our water bottles back at camp so we wouldn't have to keep up with them on the carnival rides. There are even water fountains throughout the carnival. We thought our usual bottes were too cumbersome when we had a ready supply so close, but really we were trading in the very thing we needed to sustain us."

"That's what I think anyway," said Mark. "My internal struggle has been that I felt like being separated from Jesus was inevitable for me. I felt like I was destined to end up back in the Black Water. That feeling intensified a lot when we split up, like I wasn't good enough to stay with my friends. I felt like it didn't matter if I resisted today, because I would just fail tomorrow."

"Yet you still resisted," I said encouragingly.

"I did, but I'm not sure why I did," he answered with a shake of his head. "It didn't feel like I was getting closer to Jesus or anything when I resisted. I didn't feel anything."

"I see now that we should have all stayed together from the beginning," I admitted. "We all let each other down when we went our own ways. But I have to say that I think Jesus is really delighted with you, even if you can't feel it. Sometimes being faithful to Jesus doesn't mean we feel close to him. I don't know why, but sometimes he feels far away, even when he's not. I don't know how to explain it, but I think he's very close to you right now, and sometime in the future you will look back and realize it."

"I hope your right," he said, standing up. "And I feel a lot better now that we're back together. So we better go find the others."

Rachel and I both agreed and stood to our feet. "I have no idea where Mary is," said Mark, "but I'm pretty sure Paul headed off in that direction." He pointed over his shoulder and off we went.

It didn't take us long to find the next oddity of the Valley. Instead of a Black Water pool we found a rock wall where people have carved their names into the rock. Hundreds and hundreds of names covered the wall. Higher and higher they went, at least 40 feet up. It was pretty impressive, and I wondered how long people have been climbing up there to have carved that many names. Then I noticed someone has mounted a sign to the wall that sported a picture of Jesus and a caption balloon that read, "See who can carve their name the highest."

"That's crazy," I murmured. "Who would believe that Jesus really wants us to risk our lives just to climb up there and carve our name in a rock higher than anyone can read it anyway?"

Regardless of my opinion, though, there were a dozen or so people at various stages of climbing the wall. They had all left their backpacks in a pile to the side and I spotted one I recognized.

"Hey, here's Paul's backpack," Mark said, pulling one out of the pile. I began looking closer at the climbers and spotted Paul, about twenty-five feet up and obviously in distress as his left foot floundered upward, trying to find his next foothold.

His foot caught a small outcropping and he pushed up against it, only to have it give way beneath him! He flailed but couldn't shift he weight fast enough and went sliding down. Grasping at anything his hands could find, he managed to slow his descent, but there was no stopping it. He ended up in a heap on the ground near us, dirt and gravel raining down on his head.

"What are you doing Paul?" I cried out, running over to him. "Are you OK?"

Paul looked up, taking a minute to register who exactly was talking to him. His shirt was dirty and ripped, and his arms and face were covered in minor cuts and bruises. I noted that while there was fresh blood running down from a scrape over one eye, many of his injuries had already started to scab over. How many times had he tried to climb this wall and fallen back down?

"Hi guys. Good to see you, but hang on. I'm going to climb up there and carve my name at the top," he replied matter-of-factly. "Don't worry, it will just take a minute."

I realized that this is a temptation for him reminiscent of his days at the Hall. He was driven to be the best, and he was used to succeeding. While the rest of us had been fooled by the carnival, Paul had seen through it and recognized the Black Water. And while that wasn't a temptation for him, this climbing challenge had lured him in.

"Paul, I think you need to think this through," I started. "Ask yourself why you are doing this. I mean, it really doesn't really matter if your name is up there at all, much less at the top. Nobody is reading all of these names, and no matter how high you carve your name someone will eventually go higher. I think maybe you feel like getting your name at the top will prove your worth or something, but your real worth to us is our friendship, not your performance."

He stopped and stared at the wall for a long time. "But didn't you see the sign? Jesus will be impressed if I climb the wall."

"No Paul," interjected Mark. "Jesus is never impressed with our feats or abilities. What you're really doing is playing the comparison game. You want to show that you are better than everyone else. But Jesus doesn't choose one person over another because one is better or one is worse. Jesus chooses each of us because he loves us, and our works don't have anything to do with it. This wall is a pointless distraction."

Paul stared at Mark, then looked at the wall. He looked at me, then at the wall again. Finally, he nodded. "You're right. Of course you're right. I got caught up in my own pride, and almost lost myself."

We helped him to his feet, introduced him to Rachel, and gave hugs all around.

Once Paul was rested and ready, we began to search from pool to pool for Mary and Rachel's family. It took longer than it had to find Mark or Paul, but finally Rachel pointed and said, "There's my husband!"

She ran over to one of the pools, indistinct from all the others, and we followed. She caught the attention of a man who was just climbing out of the water, and he smiled at her. We guessed that this was her husband, James. It was just as Rachel had said: he was friendly and glad to see her, but distracted by the Black Water. He didn't seem to recognize how long he had been there or be interested in meeting us. He was fixated on getting to the next pool, and seemed unable to comprehend anything else, including the loss of his sons.

He started pulling away, smiling but anxious to move on, just as Rachel had described to me. This time, though, she pulled him back and held up his water bottle.

"Honey, you're not seeing things straight. Drink this, please. It will help," she pleaded.

James stopped and stared at the bottle for a moment before recognition flashed across his face. Slowly, he reached out and took the bottle, then opened the top and drank deeply.

As he lowered the water bottle, astonishment crossed his face as he looked all around him, obviously realizing the reality of his surroundings for the first time. He sank down, weak at the knees, and fell forward into his wife's arms. Paul stepped up to help support him, guiding him over to an out-of-the-way hillside and lowering him down to the ground. Rachel sank down next to him and they held each other for several minutes, the tears flowing freely. It was a private moment, so Paul, Mark and I stepped away to give them some space.

"Where do you think Mary is?" Paul asked.

"I'm not sure," I replied. "I'm guessing the weakness that would capture her would have something to do with her past in the Hall of Good Works, but we don't know the layout of this place well enough to know what that would be."

"I think it will be something more like the rock wall than it will be a Black Water pool," added Mark. "We should look for those types of traps."

"I agree," said Paul. "When I arrived, the Black Water didn't tempt me at all, and I was actually growing bored with this place when I spotted the wall."

At that point, Rachel and James joined us, with introductions being made once again. We resumed our search as a group, not wanting anyone to get separated. We watched for Mary while Rachel and James looked for any sign of their sons.

It wasn't long before Peter, the younger boy, was spotted, and James took immediate command of the situation. Taking another water bottle from Rachel, he marched right up to Peter and insisted on a conversation. After a few minutes, the young man drank from his own water bottle and once again we witnessed the dramatic transformation of awakening.

It was encouraging to see our party growing larger and larger as we went. We still had seen no sign of Mary, though, and the knowledge that Rachel had never been able to find her oldest, Jacob, was a definite concern. Still we searched, scanning every Black Water pool and watching for other types of temptations. I knew the Valley wasn't big enough for someone to stay hidden indefinitely, but then why hadn't Rachel had any success?

James began stopping other people and asking questions about where things were, always phrasing his words as though we were in a real carnival. He learned about different attractions and rides in the Valley, and eventually became excited after talking to one elderly gentleman.

"I think I have a lead," he exclaimed, rejoining the group. "There is what that man calls a House of Good Deeds in the very center of the Valley. It sounds a lot like some sort of Hall of Good Works to me, and that is something that would attract Jacob."

"Mary too," Mark chimed in. "Let's go."

We walked more quickly now, still watching the faces of those we passed but moving intentionally towards the center of the Valley. As we approached, we saw a small building that looked very much like a miniature Hall of Good Works. Just as the man said, there was a sign posted above it with a picture of Jesus smiling next to bright letters reading, "House of Good Deeds."

We made a bee line for the door and burst through it, then came up short as we looked around. On the inside, this place looked nothing like the Hall of Good Works. It looked more like a carnival funhouse, and I wondered at the twist of reality that caused everything else to have the appearance of a carnival when it wasn't, but this to have the appearance of something substantial when it was really the only carnival-like building here.

I didn't have much time for contemplation, however, as we moved forward to start our search. Loud music and flashing lights overwhelmed our senses. The first room was a hall with mirrors covering the walls on either side, all with curves and angles to make the observer appear short, tall, fat, skinny, or just plain weird. At the end of the row was a mirror with Jesus' face painted above it. Jesus was still smiling, but next to him was a speech bubble reading, "See how you appear when I look at you…" Interested, I stepped in front of the mirror, and immediately shrank back. The image of myself in the mirror was hunched over, twisted and dripping with Black Water. My eyes were sunken in and the pasty flesh drooped off my face like it was barely hanging on. And hulking over my back was my old backpack, twice the size I remembered it. I've never seen a more wretched-looking person in all my life!

I stepped back, shocked. "That's not really what Jesus sees. You know that, right?" Paul said from behind me.

"Yeah," I said, though my voice trembled. "Yeah, I know. This is maybe what I once was, or might have become. But Jesus transformed me away from this. It's just startling to see it, you know?"

"Best to just walk on by," James said, marching through the doorway into the next room. Still, I hung back and watched each of my friends slow and stare into the mirror for a moment before moving on. It was just impossible not to look. I wondered what each of them saw, but reminded myself I really didn't need to know, because it wasn't who they were and I wouldn't want to think of them like that.

The second room was built around a narrow, hanging bridge over a dark pit. We couldn't see the bottom. The walls and ceiling were rounded, like we were walking through a tunnel, with rows of lights flashing in succession to make the room appear to be spinning. It created quite a dizzying effect. There was another sign featuring the same image of Jesus, this time with the caption, "Each room is designed to help you overcome your own weaknesses so you can be worthy of my Kingdom."

I balked at the audacity of the lie, knowing Jesus never expected us to make ourselves worthy of his Kingdom, and if he did we would never be able to succeed. Still, I felt a certain draw to completing the tasks, thinking Jesus would be pleased if I improved myself a little. Once again, I reminded myself of my experiences with Jesus, knowing that he was the one who transformed me through my trust and obedience to him, not my ability to accomplish a series of tasks. I became more like who Jesus wanted me to be when I was hiking the trails with him, helping people in need, and listening to his words of love spoken to me. And even when I failed, Jesus still looked at me with love, not disappointment or shame.

"What weakness do you think this room is supposed to fix?" asked Mark. "I didn't know equilibrium was a weakness," he added, laughing.

"It might be supposed to represent walking on the narrow path," Paul reflected. "Keep your eyes straight ahead and don't turn to the left or to the right, and you'll be ok."

"But that sounds like a worthy goal," James interjected. "Why would there be a problem with that?"

"I suspect each of these rooms will contain a worthy goal," answered Paul. "The dangers are much more subtle. For example, if the point of this test is that we must keep our eyes focused straight ahead, what do you think we should be focused on?"

"Jesus," Rachel responded without hesitation. "We keep our eyes on Jesus."

"Exactly," Paul assured her. "But what gives us the impression that Jesus is straight across this bridge?"

We all hesitated, then Peter said, "I guess it's because it is straight and narrow. And we all remember following Jesus across the bridge over the Dark Abyss. So this just looks like the right way to go in order to follow Jesus."

"That's where the danger lies," Paul said with satisfaction. "This room, this bridge, was made by someone other than Jesus, but they designed it to remind us of truths Jesus has taught us. They want us to become distracted by actually focusing on the straight and narrow path rather than focusing on Jesus. All the while, they've defined what the straight and narrow is, and what it isn't, for us, and we're playing into their hands. It's just like all these cheesy signs that claim to be the words of Jesus, but aren't really. By focusing on crossing this straight and narrow bridge, we're really focusing on ourselves and building up our own pride rather than growing closer to Jesus."

Peter added, "I doubt that making it through one of these rooms would make much of a difference in our relationship with Jesus. But if we go through room after room, we will get a little more off-center with each one, until we find ourselves back into a religious, legalistic view of Jesus without even knowing it.

"So then…we shouldn't cross the bridge?" Mark asked hesitantly.

Paul took a step forward, saying, "Oh, I think we have to cross the bridge, because that's where Mary and Jacob have gone. The key is that as we cross, we do so in complete dependence on Jesus. We let go of any pride in doing something for Jesus, even something as easy as crossing a bridge. Instead, we focus on Jesus doing something in us."

With that, Paul stepped out onto the bridge and began to walk across. He moved slowly, putting one foot down in front of the other with precision, and more than once he careened to one side or the other before regaining his footing. In any other situation, it would have been comical to watch. Once he reached the other side, he turned back towards us, beckoning us to follow.

One by one, we made our way across. When it was my turn, I stepped out onto the bridge and my whole perception changed. The bridge seemed narrower, the pit deeper, and the lights blinding. The room spun above, and I soon felt as if I was spinning too. My instinct was to step back, off the bridge. Instead I closed my eyes, blocking out the obnoxious visuals. I realized that I could do this. I mean, that I could do it by my own willpower. I could conquer the fear and dizziness and nausea that were taking hold. I didn't have to feel weak, relying on Jesus because there was no other choice. In fact, that's what I instinctively wanted to do. But then a new thought opened up inside my mind: I could choose to be weak in order to experience Jesus' power in me! Just because I could do something without him didn't mean that I should do it that way. Jesus wasn't just waiting to lend support only when I failed on my own, although that was how I had initially known him. Instead, Jesus invited me to rely on him always. It was a subtle difference that nobody else around me could see, but it made all the difference in my worldview. I took a deep breath, and prayed for God to carry me safely across. Then, just like Paul, I put one foot in front of me and walked the tightrope across the room.

Once we were all across, we turned to see what would happen next. There was a closed door in front of us, and another picture of Jesus next to it. "Congratulations!" it read. "You successfully crossed the Narrow Bridge. Have a sticker!" A small dispenser next to it was spitting out little stickers that we could take and adhere to our shirts, each one with Jesus' image and a random pithy saying. We beheld them with a mixture of amusement and frustration. Nobody took a sticker.

Peter opened the door ahead of us, and we all tumbled out into a large room. There were rows and rows of doors lining all four walls, and the room was open to allow us to see more levels with more doors above us. People moved from one door to the next with an air of busy-ness and intent. We were in a central hub for more and more "tests" like the one we had just experienced.

"What do we do now?" Mark asked. "We'll never find them just wondering around in these rooms."

"We won't have to," answered Paul. "We just have to stay here and wait, and eventually they will come to us."

We moved out into the center of the main floor, hoping to be as visible as possible and scanning the faces of the people passing by at the same time.

"Over there!" Mark exclaimed, pointing over to a corner. I don't know how he spotted her, but there was Mary huddled down against the wall. We ran over, shouting her name as we went. She looked up, and her eyes immediately filled with tears. Paul, Mark and I all tried to hug her at once, then pulled her to her feet. Her clothes were disheveled and a handful of "Jesus stickers" were slapped on her jacket, although some of them were already peeling or torn.

"You came for me," she exclaimed through her sobs. "You came for me."

"Of course we came for you," I said comfortingly. "We would never leave you." After a pause, I added, "I'm sorry we left before. I'm sorry we split up when we came to this valley."

"Me too," Mark chimed in. "That was a mistake if I ever saw one."

Once Mary had settled down, we introduced her to James, Rachel and Peter. She explained that she had been excited about entering this place, feeling a familiarity to the Hall of Good Works. She had gone through several of the tests, but each one left her feeling empty and alone. Eventually, she had given up and looked for a way out, but couldn't find one. Panicked, she had lost hope and settled into her little corner.

"Did you ask Jesus to help you?" Peter asked with a hint of accusation in his voice.

"Yes, but nothing happened."

"What do you mean, 'Nothing happened'?" Paul exclaimed, throwing up his hands. "We're here, aren't we?"

Mary let out her breath and smiled, "Yeah, I guess you are."

"Now to find Jacob," announced James, moving back towards the center of the room. We all joined him, although our original group had no idea what he looked like.

Finding Jacob took longer than finding Mary had. But eventually, Rachel spotted him exiting a room two floors above us. She began yelling to him as James and Peter began to run, taking the stairs two at a time. Once they caught his attention, he turned with a big smile on his face, and another family reunion took place.

Paul, Mark, Mary and I climbed the stairs more leisurely, letting them have their moment. We could see Jacob was an athletic young man, and his chest was covered with stickers. There must have been a hundred of them, and he had started sticking them onto the front of his jeans as well.

"But don't you see, this place is exactly what I've been looking for," he was saying excitedly as we grew close enough to hear him.

"No, Son," James said patiently. "It's not what you think it is. This isn't the life Jesus has planned for us at all."

"This is just the Hall of Good Works all over again," added Rachel, clinging to her son.

"Which is exactly why it's right," Jacob argued, stiffening against his mother's embrace. "I never wanted to leave the Hall, but you made me. Don't get me wrong, I know you guys were only doing what you thought was best. And I was too young to have any say in the matter. But now I'm older, and I'm staying here."

Rachel unclipped his water bottle from her belt and pushed it towards him, saying, "At least take your water bottle. Jesus gave it to you, remember? It will help you see the truth."

"Sorry, Mom, but it will just weigh me down. I'm making great time, and there's plenty of water fountains along the way."

James' voice rose with desperation as he argued, "Please listen to us, Son. We've been separated for too long already. You've got to come with us, to continue the journey Jesus put us on. This place is a dead end."

"Dead end? Just look what I've accomplished!" laughed Jacob, motioning to his collection of stickers. "I'm already on Level 3. And I've only been here a couple of days."

"You've been here for weeks, months even," Rachel pleaded. "And what good are all these stickers? They don't mean anything to who you really are."

"I sorry, Mom. Dad. But I've made up my mind." With that, he pulled away and disappeared into the next door without looking back. Rachel fell into her husband's arms, weeping. Peter stood a few feet away, looking lost. I went over to him and put my arm around his back.

"What do we do now?" Mary asked after a couple of minutes.

"I think there's only one thing we can do," I said. "We find the way out of here and we leave this valley. There has to be a way farther up the mountain, or Jesus wouldn't have sent us this way."

"I agree," Mark said.

James looked up from his wife, who was still crying. "We can't leave, not without our son."

"He's made up his mind and you're not going to be able to change it," Paul said soberly.

"We can try," cried Rachel.

"You're probably right," said James. "We may not be able to change his mind. But we can be here for him when his course finally runs out and he hits bottom. He'll need us more than ever then."

"I understand," Paul responded. "But I can't help but think you're compromising your own journey in the process."

"Could you do any different if it was one of your loved ones?"

"Probably not."

"I do want you to do something for me, though."

"Name it."

"Take Peter with you."

Peter started to protest, but James took a step over to him and wrapped his arms around his younger son. "You need to continue on, to find the life Jesus has for you. You won't find that here. I know it's hard, but I truly believe we will be together again soon."

Getting out of the building proved easier than we thought: especially Mary. Always thinking ahead, Paul had grabbed one of the stickers and plastered in onto the door we had used when entering the central hub. We all laughed at the picture of Jesus giving a "Thumbs Up!" with the caption, "Way to go!" It was not the way the makers of this place intended us to go, but it certainly worked.

The door wouldn't open when we tried it, but it wasn't long before someone else came through and we caught it before it closed. We quickly made our way back across the bridge, through the room of mirrors, and out into the bright sunlight.

Finding our way out of the valley was harder than we thought, however. We could see the mountain rising up above us, so we knew which way we wanted to go, generally. But there were no markings for finding the trail, and the stream had to be crossed. Much of the far side was a steep cliff that none of us had the ability to climb, so we skirted onward around the valley until the far side looked a little more inviting. The underbrush was thick over there, though, and we found ourselves wading across only to wade back when we could find no way through. We ended up doing this several times. It was very discouraging, and we eventually had to stop for the night.

The next morning, though, brought a newfound hope. When I awoke, a deer was drinking from the stream. Startled by my presence, she dashed off to one side a dozen yards then disappeared through the think growth on the other side of the water. We couldn't see the trail, but after wading across once again, we were able to crawl through and find the path she had taken. After fighting through twenty yards or so of mud and underbrush, we scrambled up a little hill and found ourselves in the clear above the river valley. From there, we found the trail, less used than it was leading up to the valley but still discernible winding its way up and up.

Epilogue

Our party of five scrambled over yet another field of jagged rocks. We were high now, and the air was thin. The trail had disappeared, but we could see the peak and pressed on for it. Paul and Mark were in the lead by fifty yards but I could see that they had stopped next to a large boulder marking the end of the rocks. "Good", I thought, "I'm certainly ready for a breather, and maybe even some lunch.

But when I caught up with them, I was surprised to find Jesus there waiting for us. Greetings and hugs were given all around, and Jesus seemed to take particular pleasure in greeting both Mary and Peter.

"I'm so proud of all of you," he said. "I've loved walking with you on this journey. If you don't mind, I'll lead the rest of the way. It's not far."

Our strength was renewed, and we pressed on, doggedly following Jesus' steps onward and upward. Up ahead, I thought I could see a grove of green trees, though we were far above the tree line. We got closer, and I was sure it was trees, but how could that be?

As we neared the grove, we could make out a figure standing at the edge, watching us. He was blazing with a bright light, reminding me of the image I had once seen of Jesus. I looked over at him, and he seemed to have a silver light around his own silhouette.

We had to get within just a few feet of the shining figure before we could make out any of his features, and then stopped dead in our tracks. There was a familiarity to him that wasn't based upon physical appearance. In fact, I couldn't say exactly what his physical appearance was. Instead, he had a familiar presence, like that of Jesus.

Jesus was now shining as brightly as the figure ahead of us, and he walked straight up to him and wrapped his arms around him in an embrace. After several moments, he turned back to us with a huge smile on his face.

"Friends," he called. "I want you to meet our Father!"

I was aware of lying down with my face to the ground, although I didn't remember falling there. I just lay there in awe of the presence before me. The Father walked over to me and kneeled down, taking my hand in his and raising me to my feet. "I am so glad you are here. Welcome to where the mountain meets the sky!"

Look for more on our Facebook page

Where the Mountain Meets the Sky

88792693R00112

Made in the USA
Columbia, SC
04 February 2018